Sandra Stoner-Mitchell

GW00496603

THE RETURN

Sandra Stoner-Mitchell

The Return

FIRST ADDITION

Copyright© 2021 Sandra Stoner-Mitchell All rights reserved.

Published with: KDP

ISBN: 9798377319900

The Author asserts his moral rights to be identified as the author of this work.

No part of this publication may be reproduced, stored in a retrieval system,

or transmitted, in any form or by any means electronic, mechanical, photocopying,

recording or otherwise, without the prior permission of the author.

This book is sold subject to the condition that it shall not, by way of trade,

or otherwise, be resold, lent hired out or otherwise circulated without the

author's prior consent, in any form of binding or cover other than that in

which it is published. This book is a work of fiction.

Sandra Stoner-Mitchell

To my husband, Graham
For all his love and
encouragement
Thankyou

The Return

1

E ven before her long slender neck arched to receive his lips on her throat, she knew what would happen yet was powerless to stop it, not when her treacherous body wanted more. She felt his breath first, then his lips followed, just brushing her tremulous skin, sending infinite ripples of exquisite, tingling sensations to her most intimate regions. Already close to the point of no return, she could no longer contain the quivering moan that escaped her dry mouth as he expertly took control.

Her cheeks flushed, heightening her fair complexion, and with eyes closed, she wallowed in the feather-light fingers that stroked and tormented. She couldn't push him away ... why would she want to? Especially as every part of her awakened body wantonly encouraged him. When he added his tongue to her delectable torture, flicking her nipples, teasing, until they were stretched, taut, igniting senses she no longer controlled, she knew she was lost.

Her fingers gripped hold of her tousled sheets as his tongue continued lustfully down past her navel sending exquisite sparks of pleasure shooting through her, turning her tingling nerve ends into a writhing mess. She wanted to bring him closer, capture his body with her thighs, but she knew, she just knew if she did....

Her husky moans filled the room as she arched her back and, reaching the point of desperation, cried out for that final abandoned moment of explosive release her fevered body craved.

Instead—she wanted to scream as she heard again that tormenting, whispery-soft chuckle of his, that abated like a drifting echo back into the natural quiet of the empty room.

'No, damn you. Come back.' Slowly, she opened her eyes. Disappointment and fury flooded her aching body once again. She breathed deeply, trying to slow her heart rate. 'Why do you keep doing this to me?' she cried out in bewilderment.

Of course, there was no answer; she was alone. At the same time, she knew she hadn't been dreaming. It was strange, she was sure she knew him—really knew him, although she didn't know how. *And* she was convinced she knew him in a sexual, intimate way—

yet, not like those fleeting moments—which was totally impossible because she was still a virgin.

She didn't even know what this phantom man looked like. He only came to torment her in her sleep. Appearing and disappearing like a heavy fog in the night. It's not as if she knew many men, and those she did know, she wasn't interested in—not in that way.

'Damn you.' She sat up and, twisting around, threw her legs over the side of the bed onto the cold linoleum flooring. She shivered, then pushed her feet into her furry slippers and padded over to the bathroom. She was in desperate need of a cold shower.

The icy water soon took care of any remaining sexual impulses … and him. Shuddering, she gave herself a good rubdown, then wrapped her striking red hair in the towel.

*****

Margot stared into the estate agent's window; the large stone house was still there. She placed a finger on the window and traced the outline. For some reason this house made her heart flutter. She shook her head. *Now you're being ridiculous.*

Every day for the past five years she'd passed by the window on her way to the bank, where she was employed as a teller, and not once looked in. There was no reason to. She didn't want to sell her flat because it was so conveniently placed in the middle

The Return

of Romford, a thriving market town and a stone's throw from where she worked. Why would she even consider moving? The mere idea of buying a house, let alone a large one so far off the beaten track, was just plain stupid.

So why was she drawn to this one? It was nice, granted, but nothing special. She sighed and turned away, meaning to continue down the road, but instead found herself opening the estate agent's door, which caused the little bell above to tinkle. No turning back now.

An elderly man, who was sitting behind the desk with his head stuck in a book, looked up. 'Good morning, my dear. How may I help you?' he asked with a bright smile that shone in his milky grey eyes. He stood, and putting his book down, indicated the chair in front of his desk. 'Please, take a seat.'

'Thank you, Mr ... Reid?' She assumed that was his name from the sign on his desk. On his nod, she continued. 'I'm interested in the white stone house you have a picture of in the window. Can you tell me something about it?'

His eyes flicked to the window. 'The stone house?' He stood up and went over to look at the display board, and seeing the only stone house there, took out two detailed leaflets from underneath the picture. 'Here we are. It must have come in yesterday when I was out of the office, although I don't remember my

Sandra Stoner-Mitchell

colleague mentioning it. Let me see now.'

He handed Margot one of the leaflets. 'It looks to be in very good order for its age. Mid-17th century. And there's indoor plumbing, but no drainage. It does have a septic tank, though.' He frowned. 'The asking price is rather low. I wonder why?'

Margot read all the details. No one had lived there for a number of years, yet from the pictures it looked as if it had been regularly maintained. The price was ridiculous though. There had to be something wrong with it. 'Is there any chance I can see it this morning? It's my day off, so it would be really convenient.'

Mr Reid looked at his watch. 'I don't see why not, Miss … ?'

'Crawford, Miss Margot Crawford.'

'Nice to meet you, Miss Crawford.' He reached out his hand, surprising Margot with his firm grip for a man of his advanced years.

'I'll just get the keys, and … ahh, the directions are on the back here. Let me see now. Yes, I know the route. That's very strange, I don't remember seeing this house before.'

He frowned and looked closer. 'I must have passed it several times, though. Oh well,' he said, shrugging, 'it must be one of those senior moments people get at my age.' He gave a little chuckle as he picked up the set of keys. 'Come, let me lock up and we can be on our way.'

The Return

The road out of town was quiet and took them through picturesque woodlands. Margot loved this road. *At least I'd enjoy my days off if I do move here.*

She smiled at the thought and sat back to enjoy the autumnal colours of the trees as they sped past … sped, being the operative word. Mr Reid wasn't hanging around.

'So, do you live around these parts?' Mr Reid asked amiably, breaking the silence.

'I live in a flat in the middle of the high street above Mandles Grocery Store. It's so handy for my needs.'

'Oh? That doesn't sound like a person wanting to change locations.'

Margot didn't answer straight away. She couldn't tell him she didn't want to move, and that this was merely a whim.

'No, you're right. I don't know what brought this on. I've passed your window every day, and never once had the inclination to move. Then a few days ago, I stopped, I'm not sure why, but I was drawn to this house. Each time I dallied to look at it, I would walk on again after a few minutes. Today, I came in.'

'A few days? I don't understand, it only went in the window yesterday.'

'No, you must be mistaken.' Margot knew she hadn't made a mistake. She glanced over at him and watched the conflicting thoughts play over his face.

She felt sorry she'd mentioned it now. 'Though, you could be right, I've had such a hectic time lately, it's possible I only saw it for the first time yesterday. But I still feel I have to see it.'

'Ah, that's most likely it. You mustn't rush through life like that. You'll understand what I mean when you reach my old age. Enjoy the moment, dear lady, enjoy the moment.'

They drove on in silence for the rest of the way, and it was quite a relief when Mr Reid pulled up outside the house.

'Here we are.' He undid his seatbelt and picked up the door keys. 'Let's take a look inside, shall we?'

Margot sat for a moment staring at the outside. The last few roses were still clinging bravely to the stems wrapped around the trellis on the front wall, giving her an insight of how it would look next summer.

There was something inviting about the place. She had to go inside. Undoing her seatbelt, she opened the car door and followed Mr Reid.

'It's lovely, much prettier than the picture,' she said, her voice so soft the words were more like a whisper on a breeze passing by.

Mr Reid was already fumbling with the keys to get the door unlocked. 'Here we go.' He stepped aside to let Margot in first.

'Thank you.' Once inside, she had the ridiculous, almost laughable, notion that she belonged here. She

The Return

moved into the first main room and was surprised by its spaciousness. As she stood there, a sudden rush of strange fragmented memories flooded her mind. Impossible memories, she knew that immediately, but they were so vivid. A man, tall, straight back, but she couldn't see his face. She saw herself, standing in front of him. Then the vision disappeared.

Shaking her head. She accused herself of an overactive imagination. She grinned. Moving on, she went through all the rooms, pleasantly surprised at how well maintained they were for a property of this age. The walls were all painted white, but that was something she could change … put her own stamp on the place. She grinned. *It sounds like you've decided to move in, my girl.*

Standing there, still smiling, Margot had the sudden notion she wasn't alone. She wasn't frightened, far from it, if anything she found it rather comforting. Obviously, a house of this age was going to have its ghosts. It was really quite nice.

It was as if the house knew her, too. Margot then had the distinct feeling of someone wrapping invisible arms about her, caressing her, breathing on the back of her neck. Closing her eyes, she suddenly had the most extraordinary, inconceivable notion flash through her mind—this had once been her home, and now? Now it was time for her return … and he was waiting.

2

Wasting no time, Margot asked Mr Reid if they could go straight to her flat so he could give her a quick valuation for a speedy sale.

'I no longer do that side of it, Miss Crawford, but by the time we get back, my colleague should be in the office. We can see if he has an hour free.'

Satisfied with that, Margot sat back and began mentally walking through the old house again. Although she couldn't explain it, she knew she belonged there.

Mr Reid's colleague was on the phone when they walked in. He raised a hand in greeting and, after a few more minutes, he finished the call. He looked up and smiled. 'Hi there…?'

The Return

'This is Miss Crawford, Kevin, she's interested in buying Holton House in Braishfield, but needs a valuation on her property before she makes an offer. Is it possible you can fit her in today? She only lives across the road above Mandles.'

Kevin looked at his watch. 'Actually, that will fit in fine with me. That was Mr Copson on the phone. They want to go ahead and put their property on the market. I have a couple of hours to spare before I go and take photos. Would it be convenient right now?' he asked, putting the question to Margot.

'Yes. Thank you.' Margot smiled, although her relief and excitement were diminished by a smidgen of trepidation. She took a deep breath to calm her nerves.

The valuation was a nice surprise and Kevin told her it would be easy to sell given its position and the surrounding area. Without further ado, she told him to go ahead.

They went back to the office and Kevin left Mr Reid to take all her details. Because of Holton House's ridiculously low price, Margot didn't bother bartering, but told him to go ahead with the purchase. Her only worry would be if someone else put in a higher bid before her flat sold.

The following days went by with Margot experiencing an influx of mixed emotions. When she was away from the house, she questioned her sanity;

why was she doing this? Yet when she went to have another look at the house, she was impatient to move in.

She couldn't deny the pull. This was where she belonged, and yet.... *Perhaps when it's truly mine, these stupid niggling doubts will disappear.*

It was while she was having yet another look around, she heard a crash. The sound, like something falling onto the floor and followed immediately by a muffled cry, had Margot standing stock still. *What do I do?* Slowly, she turned her head and looked around for a weapon of some sort. Spying a poker leaning by the empty fire grate she tiptoed over and very gently picked it up.

Once in the wide reception hall, she saw a door ahead that was slightly ajar, and moved towards it. A shuffling movement came from inside and, with the poker held tight and secure in her hand giving her much needed confidence, she slowly pushed the door open.

'Oh, mercy me. You fair made me poor old heart drop to the pit of me belly.' A middle-aged lady, who was standing in the middle of the room holding a cloth in one hand, and patting her heart with the other, stared at Margot and laughed.

'I'm sorry, but …' Margot lowered the poker and stared at the woman standing in front of her. She frowned, trying to think where she'd seen her before.

The Return

The sun chose that moment to peep from behind the clouds, shining through the kitchen window to envelop the woman and give her an ethereal glow.

'Who *are* you?' Margot whispered, then blinked as the spell was broken by invisible fingers snatching the sun back again, hiding it behind the darkening storm clouds.

'Why, I's Bessie, the housekeeper. I's been keeping the old house neat and tidy while it's been empty. Didn't they tell you about me? Hmm? I's just been in the garden, cutting some herbs.'

As if to prove it, she bent down and picked up the metal bowl. Seeing a few herbs scattered on the floor, Margot realised the fallen bowl had been the cause of the noise she'd heard.

'I's going to hang them to dry,' she said, with a smile that lit her eyes. After placing the bowl on the table, she wiped her hands down her apron.

'Ah, that explains a lot. Hello Bessie, I'm Margot, and, hopefully, I'll soon be the new owner.'

'Yes, I know. I's been expecting you.'

That was strange. 'Ah, of course, Mr Reid would have let you know.'
Bessie's eyes twinkled as she smiled, but she didn't say a word.

*****

Everything happened so fast after that, Margot

barely had time to catch her breath. Her flat sold the same week, and the contracts were all signed within a fortnight. Three people had put in an offer for her flat, but in the end, one of them offered her cash saying he needed to move in as soon as possible. That clinched the deal.

After the completion, Margot was surprised to see how much money she had left. Her flat sold for far more than the price of the house, in fact, she was able to pay cash. With no mortgage, she had enough money left to buy a small car. It had suddenly occurred to her that she would no longer be able to walk to work.

The house came fully furnished, and because she didn't want to change anything, the buyer of her flat had negotiated a good price for the furniture she left behind.

Now, here she was, standing in her new home, keys in her hand, and totally bemused. In just over two weeks she had moved from her perfectly placed flat, into a house that…

'Into a house that made you buy it.' There was no other way she could explain it. 'So, why am I here?' She waited. 'Really, Margot? You're asking the house and expecting it to answer?' She shook her head and grinned. 'They'll be locking you up if you're not careful.'

'No, Margot, the house knows you belong here …

The Return

You knows it, too.'

Margot spun around. 'Oh, Bessie, you scared the life out of me.' Then she chuckled. 'You did that on purpose to get your own back on me, didn't you?'

Bessie's eyes twinkled, and again, Margot wondered where she knew her from. Those twinkling eyes were so expressive, yet didn't reveal the secrets hidden behind them. 'If there's nothing you want me to do, dearie, I'll leave you to settle in. I'll be back in the morning.'

It didn't take her long to unpack her cases and hang her clothes in the wardrobe. The next thing to do was make up her bed. She'd brought a new duvet, which she thought she'd need at this time of the year, and three sets of Egyptian cotton sheets. Although there were clean sheets and blankets in the ottoman at the bottom of the bed, she hadn't wanted to sleep in bedding that someone else had used.

In the kitchen she stood for a moment to see where she'd put her microwave. There was no way she'd leave that behind. Her television, radio and laptop would have to wait until an aerial could be fitted before she could use them.

The last item to be put away was her antique silver cutlery. A family heirloom, the set had been passed down from her great-great-great-grandmother. Each generation had sworn never to sell them.

Now she'd found a home for everything, there was

nothing left to do. *Bessie has done a great job of keeping it nice and clean. I must remember to ask her tomorrow if she'd consider staying on.*

Because there wasn't a shower, Margot decided to relax for a while in a nice hot bath. She'd bought her candles, and her favourite scented bath oils. Going into her bedroom, she undressed and tied her long hair up into a bun, clipping it in place on the top of her head. Hanging one of her large soft towels on the rail by the door, she gingerly stepped into the full bath of soft, perfumed water.

She gave a deep contented sigh as she lay back and closed her eyes, allowing all her doubts to slip away with the help of the flickering candles and their softly scented glow.

As Margot drifted deeper into a warm relaxed state, she had that familiar feeling of no longer being alone. She knew it was him. Her amorous, mysterious ghost. For a moment, she didn't know whether to be pleased or angry but some irritation swept through her.

How the hell did he know I was here? Is he stalking me? A splutter of laughter collided with a cough at that ridiculous thought. But when she felt his breath on her neck, the laughter drained away.

Although still incredibly seductive, something about him had changed. It was the way he touched her, there wasn't the urgency he'd always shown before.

But it's more than that it's ... mmm, that's nice ... mmm, ... what do I care? He's still pushing all the right buttons.

A shudder of excitement rippled through her as he gently brought about feelings she'd never known before, but which both thrilled and embarrassed. She kept her eyes closed tight; fearful he'd leave if she opened them.

She held her breath, silently pleading for more as she felt his gentle fingers moving slowly and deliberately over her taut stomach... Then he stopped. It was then she knew what was different. *He's going to leave. For good?* As if he'd read her mind, she felt him move away.

'Soon, my sweet Meg, we'll soon be together ... forever...'

Margot's eyes snapped open. Her body spasmed violently, causing her legs to thrash about in her panic to push herself up and out of the bath, sending a tidal wave that doused the candles before it poured over the side. Oblivious of the puddle she was standing in, she grabbed her towel and wrapped it around herself protectively.

That was the first time she'd actually heard him speak, apart from his tormenting laugh. Normally she heard him in her head ... *and what did he mean?*

'Who the hell are you? I am not your Meg.' she screamed out, her voice shaking. 'I'm Margot … I'm Margot, not Meg.' Her final words slipped out as a whisper.

The Return

3

The following morning, Margot was awakened from a refreshing dreamless sleep by the sun streaming through her window. Yawning, she pulled the duvet back and scrambled out of bed. It seemed her decision not to dwell on the amorous ghost any more, to put him right out of her mind, had worked.

Today, she wanted to tackle the attic, but after taking a quick look, decided she would ask Bessie if she'd mind giving her a hand. Bessie had been more than happy to continue as housekeeper, which pleased Margot no end. She was a bright character and fun to have around. An added bonus was her immense knowledge regarding the history of the house.

'I's not been up here for a long time,' Bessie told her as they both stood looking at all the stuff. 'Some of this is junk, but some might be worth keeping.'

'Let's start with the trunks. Who knows,' Margot said, laughing, 'there might be some hidden treasure in one of them.'

They both worked at a steady pace, Bessie asking if she wanted to keep or throw away certain items as she held them up. After an hour of this, Margot realised it was going to take a lot longer than she'd first envisioned.

Looking around at the trunks still to be checked, she made a decision. 'Let's open that big trunk over in the corner, and then we'll call it a day.' Margot forged a path through odd pieces of furniture and children's toys to get to it.

This one wasn't going to reveal its contents as easily as the others had. 'I need a hammer to knock this lock off,' Margot said. 'Wait here. I'll go and get one.'

She was soon back and, giving the lock a few hard knocks, they gave a cheery thumbs up as it fell away.

'Well, here's your hidden treasure,' Bessie said. She'd watched Margot's face change to surprise and grinned at her gawping at the contents. 'I's thinking that is a wedding dress.'

Margot sat back on her haunches, staring at the dress with its beautiful diamond headdress. When memories of events that couldn't possibly have happened vividly assaulted her mind, she tried to turn away, but couldn't.

She saw herself wearing this dress and walking into a church, but the only part of the groom she could see was his back. Then the aisle seemed to stretch, taking the groom farther and farther away from her. She saw his arms, reaching for her, but he was just a blur now, and too far away for her to grab them.

Suddenly the scene changed, she was now dressed to go horse-riding. This time, though, she was crying and shouting at someone just out of sight. Next, she watched herself grab hold of the reins and, leaping expertly into the saddle, she urged the horse forward into a gallop.

Margot's whole body shivered. She leapt to her feet and slammed the trunk shut. *That wasn't me, no way. It couldn't be.*

Bessie jumped up beside her. Taking hold of Margot's arm, she whispered, 'You look like you've seen a ghost.'

Not wanting to spend any more time in the attic, and not wanting to share what had just happened to her, Margot shook her head dismissively.

'Nothing, I just felt someone walk over my grave,' she told Bessie. Then forced a smile as she turned to leave. 'Come on, I think we've done enough up here for today. Let's go and make some coffee.'

Bessie grimaced and shook her head. 'Coffee? No thanks, I's been told it tastes really bitter, and it's not good for men because … well …' Bessie blushed to the roots of her hair.

'What, Bessie? Why is it bad for men? That's news to me.'

Bessie lifted her head. 'I's been told it stops them from making babies.'

Margot was flabbergasted, and much to Bessie's astonishment, she laughed.

'Oh Bessie, I needed a giggle, and you've just given me one. Who told you that? It's just not true. As for the bitter taste, there are some like that, but I prefer the milder, smooth coffee.   Oh, my dear lady, I insist you try it, I know you'll enjoy it. Come. Let's go down to the kitchen.'

A short while later, both the women were sitting at the table, looking at the cups filled with coffee. 'Go on, then … try it.' Margot encouraged.

Bessie lifted her cup and brought it to her nose and sniffed. 'Smells okay.' She then took a tentative sip … followed by another. Her face lit up. 'I's liking this.'

'I thought you would. You can buy several types of coffee; this one is my favourite.'

'Oh, well then, you'd better be showing me the others … just so's I know which one I like best.' She grinned, and continued taking small sips of the hot liquid.

Later, after Bessie had left for the day, Margot

25

The Return

decided to check out more of her new home. She wanted to get rid of the images she'd seen of herself up in the attic. First on her list, was to learn what else had been included in the price, apart from the furniture. It was a lot more than she'd seen when Mr Reid had shown her around.

As Margot moved around the house, discovering more and more antiques, many obviously worth a mint, it made the price she paid for the house even more ridiculous.

Who owned this house before I did? Why would they leave all these lovely pieces here? It doesn't make sense.

There was one other thing that struck her about the house; there appeared to be more rooms than she'd previously seen. *What is it about this house?*

The room she was in now had evidently been the library. The shelves, although quite spartan, had a few books on them.

At least I'll have something to read while I'm waiting for the television and the Internet to be connected. There was a highly polished writing desk under the window, unquestionably placed so the writer could gaze out at the lovely view of the garden.

Bessie's done a wonderful job caring for this house. Everything is spotless. I'm glad she accepted my offer to stay. Now, what's inside the desk?

Margot sat on the chair and opened one of the

cupboards underneath the desk, discovering bottles of whisky, brandy, and port. With three elegant crystal glasses, each selected for whichever drink was chosen, Margot surmised this person drank alone.

'Why would anyone keep alcohol in a writing desk?' Margot lifted out each bottle and saw the port was the only bottle unopened. The whisky was almost empty, whilst the brandy was three-quarters full.

Above the cupboard were two drawers. Margot opened one and found writing paper, four fountain pens and ink. The other drawer was more interesting. This revealed a diary and a well-thumbed family Bible. She picked up the Bible first and carefully opened the fragile cover. *Hmm, this looks like it might give me some clues.*

The first two pages revealed a list of names and dates. Although the names had faded, a few were still legible, along with some of the dates.

'This must have belonged to a family who once lived here,' she murmured softly, then frowned as she looked closer at the last few documented names, and the dates of their entries.

'1886. Well, that can't be right.'

Confused, Margot squinted trying to read one of the names that stood out, and recoiled … Meg. 'My amorous ghost's lost love.' Looking closer, she tried to make out her surname, but couldn't, but she could read her date of birth, 28-10-1857 died 11-11-1886.

The Return

Meg was only twenty-nine when she died … the same age Margot would be soon. Not only that, they both shared the same birth date but a hundred and thirty-five years apart.

And my birthday is in four weeks' time…

4

Feeling quite cold now, Margot took the Bible and diary into the kitchen so she could get warm and make a hot drink. Discovering there *had* been a woman named Meg living in this house, was bad enough, but to learn they'd shared birth dates, well, *that* had *really* given Margot the heebie-jeebies.

If only my internet was connected, I might have been able to trace her, or some of the previous occupiers. I'm sure this house is old enough to have been mentioned somewhere, probably in the Doomsday Book.

Margot stared at the Bible and diary, but was loath to open either now. The Bible had given her a shock, and the diary was bound to bring out more surprises.

The Return

She'd had enough of those today. 'I don't know what I'll do if I discover it's Meg's diary. It will be far too personal if she is my ghost's lost love.'

Especially after what he's been doing to me. Margot's shoulders slumped. *No, that wouldn't do at all. I'll wait until Bessie comes tomorrow. She might have heard something about this Meg person.*

Satisfied she'd come up with a good enough reason not to read any more, she put the two books on one of the kitchen's many shelves, then whipped up a mushroom and onion omelette for her supper.

*****

The following morning Margot was brought rudely out of a deep sleep by the sound of a noisy cock, crowing its head off, right under her bedroom window. Her first thought was to cover her head with her pillow in the hope it would muffle the sound, but then she remembered Bessie would arrive at eight-thirty. With a groan, she struggled out of bed and, pulling on her warm dressing gown, started getting ready for the day ahead.

Margot was sitting at the kitchen table, munching on a piece of toast, when the kitchen door opened. 'Good morning, Bessie. My goodness, you look half frozen. Help yourself to coffee; it's freshly made. It will help thaw you out.'

The hour hand on the clock had moved onto the

half-hour. Margot marvelled at how her new friend always managed to arrive bang on time.

Bessie didn't need to be told twice. 'Yous right about that. I's colder'n Jack Frost's fingers.' She dropped her bag on one of the chairs and, after removing her coat, scarf, thick gloves and woolly hat, took a cup out from the cupboard. 'So's, what do you want me to be doing today?'

Margot waited until she'd finished her toast, and Bessie was sitting at the table with her coffee, before she replied.

'I would very much like to pick your brains about the history of this house, and its previous owners, if you wouldn't mind?'

Bessie shrugged. 'Why would I mind? You go right ahead.'

'Thanks. I went into the library, or study, whatever you want to call it, and found an old family Bible and a diary. Do you know anything about a woman called Meg?'

Bessie gave her a quizzical look, so Margot carried on, 'I'd quite understand if you don't. Apparently, she died a long time ago, one hundred and thirty-five years ago, to be precise. It's just, well, you seem to know a lot about the history of this house, which led me to wonder...' She let the sentence hang.

Bessie's face remained neutral, not giving Margot any clues. 'Meg? That's a long ways back.' She

The Return

seemed to give the question some thought. 'Now why would you be asking about someone living that long ago?'

She picked up her cup and took another sip, not once breaking eye contact with Margot. 'I's sure this old place has its fair share of ghosts … Oh. Is that what this is about, has you seen a ghost? Oh, mercy me.'

Margot laughed, 'No, I've not seen any ghosts,' *Only felt one.* 'I know it sounds funny, but it was … Okay, here goes, when I looked inside the Bible, I could see it had been passed down through the generations of the same family. One of the last entries was of a lady named Meg, I couldn't read her surname, but the strange thing is, she was born the same day I was, and died in 1886.'

'I's can see why that would be spooky, but I's sure that is just a coincidence. Or do you feel it could be more?'

'You wouldn't believe me if I told you,' Margot said sadly. 'Do you know anything about her?'
Bessie reached over and patted Margot's hand. 'Why don't you try me? I's might understand more'n you think.'

Their eyes locked. Again, Margot felt that distinct sense of familiarity. Not only was she certain she'd met Bessie before, but she had a strong belief she could trust her, as well.

Sandra Stoner-Mitchell

The bank. Of course, that's where I must have seen her.

Now that mystery was solved to her liking, Margot stood up, went over to the coffee-pot and refilled her cup. The piping hot liquid sent wafts of the delicious aroma into the room. Drawing it in with a deep sigh, she went back to the table before taking a sip.

'A few months ago, while I still lived in my flat, I started having the craziest dreams,' Margot said, hesitating a moment. 'A man comes into my room just before sunrise. I feel I know him, which is freaky, because I'm absolutely sure I don't. Does that make sense?'

'Yes. Go on.'

Margot looked at Bessie again, then continued, 'Well, he's really … romantic, he makes me feel things I've never felt before.'

'You's not the first lady to have such dreams. So, what makes this so different?'

'Everything. Everything that has been happening to me only started when he haunted my dreams.' Margot huffed. 'I'd never wanted to move from my flat, it was a nice home and very convenient for my work. But the moment I saw this house in the estate agent's window, I knew I belonged here. How insane is that? Now it gets crazier. My dreams have continued here; this man followed me.'

Bessie smiled. 'The man didn't 'follow' you,

dearie, you brought him with you.'

Margot took a deep breath. 'I suppose … and I would have agreed with you had he not spoken to me. He never said a word back in my flat.' Margot looked down at her hands wrapped around her cup.

'He said we'd soon be together, forever. And this is the weirdest part, he keeps calling me Meg. And now I find out that someone named Meg lived here, and died. I think he believes I'm this Meg, his lost love. Am I going crazy?'

Bessie was quiet for a few minutes. Her facial expressions were unreadable, but her eyes told Margot she knew something. She waited.

'You said you found a diary? Have you read it?'

'No. I … I wanted to wait until I'd spoken to you.'

'Shall we read it together?'

'That's what I hoped you'd say.' Margot shook her head. 'I've never been, what kids say, a scaredy-cat.' She grinned. 'But this has really spooked me. I've got it into my head this diary is going to reveal more stuff that I'm not sure I can handle. At least, not on my own.'

Margot went over and took the Bible and the diary off the kitchen shelf. 'The Bible looks to be very old. I didn't look to see the first entry, only the last few which included Meg's birth and death.'

'Sometimes families are like that. But I think there was more to it than that. Let's take a look at the diary.'

Bessie pushed it towards Margot, and sat back.

The cover was in better condition than the Bible, which was understandable. It had a picture of a horse and dog on the front, and the sea on the back. Margot carefully opened the cover, and shuddered.

'No, that's not possible.' She stared at the passage, before reading aloud, *"This Diary Belongs To Meg Crawford."* What's going on here?' Margot looked up at Bessie, and saw nothing, no shocked expression, just her usual unruffled look.

'Now don't you be getting all upset like. There be's more'n you with that name. Let's read the next page.'

Margot automatically turned the page, and stared at the neat script writing. Not like her scrawling writing at all. She took a deep breath and calmed down a bit.

"January 1st 1878

I am so excited. Papa has agreed to Miles' request to marry me. I am the luckiest girl in the land. All my friends will be so envious.'"

'Miles? Is that the name of my ghost?' Margot looked up at Bessie, but only received a shrugged as a response. She continued turning the pages. Most were just excited young girl's ramblings.

Bessie sat quietly watching as Margot turned the pages, skimming the entries.

"April 10th 1878

The Return

My wedding is getting closer, June 4th. Why does time go so slow? My dress is almost finished and it looks so lovely."'

Margot looked up at Bessie. 'I'll go forward to her wedding day. So far, it's just a young lady's excitement at her coming betrothal.'

Bessie still said nothing, just nodded.

Margot frowned. Something was wrong, she could sense it. Slowly turning to June the fourth, her frown deepened. There was nothing. She turned the pages back to the last entry. May 25th.

'"I'm never going to marry now. If I can't have Miles. My life is over."'

Margot turned back more pages, but there was nothing, no explanation. Not since May the tenth. The pages before were still the excited ramblings of a girl in love and waiting to be married.

'I don't understand. What could have happened?' She stared at Bessie, totally befuddled. 'What could possibly have changed that Meg didn't marry Miles? It doesn't make sense.'

Still, Bessie stayed silent, just lowered her head, but not before Margot saw the sadness in her eyes.

'What, Bessie?'

5

The long silence felt more like minutes to Margot, rather than the few seconds it was in real time. Bessie knew things, but for some reason known only to her, she didn't seem keen to share them.

'Bessie?' Margot reached out to touch her hand. 'What is it? Please, Bessie, why won't you tell me?'

'Things are never what they seem,' Bessie told her gently.

'Yeah, so I've recently been discovering.' Margot waited, hoping Bessie would continue. When that didn't happen, she sighed. Her patience was waning. 'What is it? I've told you what's been going on in my life, and I'm sure you know things that I don't. Perhaps if you share them with me, I'll be better able

The Return

to understand.'

When Bessie lifted her face, Margot was shocked to see her eyes were moist. 'Bessie? For heaven's sake, talk to me.'

She started to pull her hand back, but Bessie held it tight, sending a most peculiar feeling shooting through her. It was then Margot knew her life was going to change. How? She didn't know. More to the point, was she ready for whatever was coming?

Bessie sat up straight, the sudden determined look on her face was telling Margot she'd come to a decision. 'I's going to tell you Mistress Meg's story. It's a sad one.'

'So, you *do* know about her. Why didn't you just tell me?'

'I's telling you now,' she snapped back, and then apologised when Margot flinched. She drained her cup, then held it out. 'I's going to need another coffee,' she said, with a fleeting smile.

'Goodness, what you'll do to drag it out.' Margot teased. Taking both their cups to the sink, she rinsed them out. 'I'll make a fresh pot.'

Once Bessie had her cup of coffee in her hands, she lifted it to her nose and, closing her eyes, sniffed the aroma. 'I's do love that smell.' After taking another sniff, she returned the cup to the table and looked into Margot's eyes. Her face softened. 'I's be thinking it's time you knew, anyways.'

'Time I knew? That sounds ominous.' Margot gave a nervous chuckle.

'No, it's nothing for you to be worried about. Are you ready to hear Mistress Meg's story?'

Margot felt excitement mixed with uncertainty, but nodded. 'Yes, I'm ready.'

'Good. It were in May, three weeks before the wedding were supposed to happen, Mistress Meg's father shot his self in the head.'

Margot spluttered on the coffee she'd just taken a sip of. 'For heaven's sake, Bessie. You don't mess about with gradual lead ups when you tell a story, do you? Why on earth did he do that? How do you know this?' Margot couldn't get her head around this unexpected development.

'I's knows a lot about this house and the people in it. You will, too. Now, do you want me to carry on?'

Margot shook her head, then nodded. 'Yes, please do.'

'It were Lady Crawford who found him. Her having a weak heart didn't help. The stress were awful. But that weren't the worst of it, mercy me, no.' Bessie's eyes glazed over for a moment.

'It was after the funeral, just before the will were s'posed to be read. Their solicitor wasn't at all happy, but it were left to him to tell Lady Crawford and Mistress Meg there weren't nothing left for Lord Crawford to leave them. That they would have to

The Return

leave their house and everything in it. That's how they found out about his Lordship's gambling habit. He'd lost everything. What a scandal that were. It hit those high society snobs like a tidal wave.'

'I've heard how gamblers can end up bankrupt, not only losing their homes, but sometimes their families, as well. They're desperately hoping the next bet will solve all their problems, but it rarely does. Addiction destroys so much,' Margot said.

'That's right. And back in them days, if'n you couldn't pay, you'd be put in the debtors' prison till you could. His Lordship wouldn't't've lasted long in one of them. I's heard they were awful places, 'specially for a gentleman. As for Mistress Meg and Lady Crawford, theys were left destitute.'

Margot kept quiet. What she was learning had left her shaken. 'What happened to Lady Crawford and Meg?'

Bessie shrugged, picked her cup up and took a sip. 'Well, for a start, the wedding was off. Miles couldn't marry Meg. Even though, had it been up to him, he would've. He loved Mistress Meg, but his father, Lord Brandon, forbade it. The scandal would've ruined his family, too.'

'Well, what a poor specimen of a man Miles turned out to be.'

'It weren't his fault, Mistress Meg knew that. Miles bought her this house, and made sure she and her mother was well looked after. As it were, Miles never married. I's thinking he were waiting for his father to die. But Meg died before that happened.'

Margot took advantage of the silence that followed. 'Bessie? You … I can't help but think … but … Bessie, it sounds very much as if you were there, that you knew Meg and Miles personally. But that can't be right, can it? So, either you're a ghost, or … something else?' She finished in a flurry of embarrassment at such a ridiculous thought.

Bessie shook her head and gave a mysterious smile. 'Anyone can find out what's been happening in the past if they looks for it.'

Although she knew that to be true, Margot didn't believe this was the case with Bessie.

But the alternative just isn't possible … is it? But then again, if Miles is a ghost, what's to stop Bessie from being one, too? Perhaps she's helping him. Surely, she couldn't feel so much sadness just by reading a history book, could she? It was all crazy. Okay, I'll let it go for now.

'So, do you know how Meg died? According to the diary, it was eight years later. She was very young.'

'She were murdered.' Bessie retorted vehemently, as her face turned a livid red.

'What? How? Why do you think she was murdered? This is getting worse by the minute.'

'It's been written that she had an accident. Her

saddle slipped and Mistress Meg fell off'n broke her neck. Of course, that's the story everyone was told. They hushed it up. It weren't surprising; money can talk a lot louder'n the truth, you know, especially as the doctor was a friend of Lord Brandon's. Mistress Meg always checked her saddle was on properly. If'n you was to ask me, something had been done to make that saddle slip.'

Margot remembered the images that had flashed through her head yesterday. She'd been Meg. The argument she appeared to be having, how upset she was, and the way she'd galloped off on the horse.

If that was really me, was that when I died? Don't be so stupid Margot. How could that possibly have been me?

'This is a lot to take in, Bessie. Why would Miles' father have Meg murdered all those years later? He'd stopped the marriage from taking place, so she couldn't have brought shame to the family. Although that still rankles with me.'

'I 'spect it were because Miles carried on seeing her and his Lordship found out. And I 'spect it were Richard who told him.'

'Richard? Who the heck was he?'

'He were Mistress Meg's brother. He weren't right in the head, if'n you ask me. Richard blamed his mother for his Lordship's death. All his life he was expecting to be the next Lord Crawford with all the trappings that came with it. And then he discovers he had nothing. Only a title attached to his father's shame.'

'And?' Margot encouraged when Bessie remained quiet.

'Well, Richard had a terrible row with his mother the day after Lord Crawford shot his self. What with her weak heart, well, she were never the same after that. Poor Meg was left with an invalid mother, and soon to have her home taken away.'

'That poor lady. In one day, she went from a happy young bride-to-be, getting ready for her wedding, to losing her father and the man she loved.'

'They managed to keep Mistress Meg's whereabouts a secret for nearly eight years. Then Miles put on a party for her birthday, and a few trusted friends was invited. It were only days later that she had that so-called accident. Miles were beside his self with grief.'

Margot's mind flew back and forth over the dates in her mind. 'If she was twenty-nine when she died, which is how old I'll be in four weeks' time, that would mean fourteen days after my birthday … is the anniversary of Meg's death.'

Bessie picked up her cup and finished her coffee. 'Yes. That's right, just forty-two days. Not long now.'

The way Bessie spoke sent a shiver of expectancy down her spine. Margot looked straight into her eyes,

The Return

trying to reach the answer to the question pulsating in her mind.

Why have I got this strange feeling that Meg's story has something to do with me?

Sandra Stoner-Mitchell

6

The time came when Margot had to return to work. The week's holiday she'd taken to settle in was up. She'd expected to feel pleased about going back, given the stress of the last week. It had been a tad different from what she'd thought, to say the least. Margot liked her life to follow a routine, and, even more, she liked to have some sense of normality to go with it.

I can honestly say, hand on heart, I haven't had a moment's peace since I stepped over the threshold of this house. So why am I feeling ... nervous? That's crazy, why would I be nervous about going back? I enjoy my job at the bank. Get a grip, Margot.

Bessie's revelations over the last weekend had unsettled her. She knew this was ridiculous, but

The Return

nevertheless, she couldn't shake off the feeling something was going to happen, and soon. What was worse, Margot still believed she was involved. But how? She didn't know.

I have to get back to work. These crazy thoughts are doing my head in.

Bessie had taken the day off, saying there were things she needed to do. Not that an explanation had been necessary, Bessie hadn't taken a day off since Margot moved in.

She took a last look at her hair and make-up before heading downstairs. After flopping around in her tracksuit and slippers all week, she almost felt overdressed in her charcoal grey, knee-length, pencil skirt, teamed with a crisp-white cotton blouse and jacket. But the bank had rules, and one of them was to look smart.

Tucking her handbag under her arm, Margot picked up her car keys and headed down the hall to collect her coat.

Just as she reached out to open the front door, the idea of leaving her home left her with a sudden irrational feeling of anxiety. She stood in front of the door, her fingers on the handle ready to open it, but she couldn't.

Her hand began to shake, beads of sweat pricked her forehead, and a sudden feeling of nausea made her swallow hard. She took some deep breaths, trying to slow the rapid pounding of her heart.

What the hell is wrong with me? This is ridiculous. Don't panic, you'll be fine.

Her arm dropped to her side, but the shakes didn't stop. She tried to force herself forward, but her feet felt like they were set in concrete. Now scared witless, a sharp sensation pounded in her chest, causing her to gasp and double over in pain.

Am I having a heart-attack? At my age? Oh, dear God, help me. What do I do?

Then, those familiar invisible arms slid around her waist, wrapping her protectively, soothing her. She could almost believe he was solid as she unfurled herself, her pains mysteriously gone.

'It's all right, Meg, I'm here. I'll always be just a whisper away.' His soft husky voice, seeming to come from an ethereal world, felt like balm to an open wound. Margot released a sigh of relief, all fear forgotten. She didn't even mind him calling her Meg anymore. Perhaps it was silly, but somehow the name seemed to belong to her now.

The feel of him faded; he was leaving again. Margot felt that same emptiness she'd become used to whenever he left her. Now able to move, she hung her coat back up and walked into the kitchen. She sat, put her elbows on the kitchen table, and rested her chin in the palms of her hands.

'Miles,' she said his name lightly, wanting to hear

The Return

how it sounded spoken with her voice. She was surprised to discover how, by saying his name aloud, it made her feel safe. It felt familiar, as if she used it a lot so she repeated it, liking the sound.

Enough of this foolishness. I have to get to work. But she didn't move. *For heaven's sake, Margot. What's the matter with you? You have to work. How can you pay your bills if you don't?*

'The simple fact is, you can't. So, stop acting childish and go to work.' This time, Margot grabbed her keys and coat, then marched up to the door. Taking a deep breath, she gritted her teeth and opened it. Once outside, another wave of nausea hit her hard.

'I can't do this.' Spinning on her heel, she went back inside and slammed the door behind her. Now the tears were falling as she dropped her coat and bag on the floor and rushed upstairs to her bedroom. 'This is crazy.'

Slowly, Margot changed her clothes, putting on her jogging bottoms, top, and trainers. Then, pulling her hair into a ponytail, she took out a woollen hat, having made up her mind to go for a run.

She did some warm-up stretches, then raced down the stairs and straight outside.

Well, that was easy. She stopped, turned around and looked back at the house. 'You knew I wasn't going to work this time, didn't you? That's why you let me out. What the hell is it with you?' Margot rolled her eyes and shook her head. 'And, what is it with me, talking to a house.' With another shake of her head, Margot set off.

Running up to the road and turned left, away from the town. The cold air kept her mind on the road ahead, and off all the mysterious things that had been happening to her lately.

The road was quiet, since there was no traffic at this time of the day. Only the sound of the pigeons broke the silence, helping her to relax and calm her shredded nerves.

The trees were rapidly losing their leaves now, scattering a red and gold blanket all over the ground below. Margot marvelled at the way Nature helped keep the seedlings and saplings in the earth from freezing.

At the top, clinging to the bare branches of some trees, she could easily see huge bunches of mistletoe. The holly was heavy with bright red berries, giving the birds their winter feed. This was what the doctor ordered to lift her spirits again.

I'll give my manager a call, tell him I'm not well. I'm sure I'll be fine tomorrow.

Rounding the corner, Margot saw the old village church ahead, and decided to look inside. The gate was made in such a way to keep the sheep in the graveyard and out of harm from the road. Her feet crunched on the gravel path that led straight to the

The Return

church door. It was locked.

It was so peaceful here, Margot walked around to the side of the church where the gravestones stood. Some were crumbling, some had cracks, all looked noticeably in need of repair. The few new headstones stood out like sentinels, protecting the older graves.

I wonder if Meg and Miles are buried here. She looked behind her to see if anyone was watching. *Why would anyone be watching you? Why would you even think that.? You really are losing it.* Margot shook her head and carried on.

Some of the names had long since faded; others were covered with lichen. Margot looked at the dates of some that were still evident and, remembering the year of Meg's death, calculated her grave would be somewhere at the back.

Moving slowly around, she was saddened at how many children were buried here. Some from the plague; others didn't say. Some only had the birth and death dates, no name.

She moved farther over, towards where she thought Meg would be buried. It was when she was nearing the hedgerow that she began to feel strange. Margot stopped.

'I's thought you'd be at work by now.'

Margot spun around; not having heard a sound, she'd been surprised to hear Bessie's voice, and astonished to see her standing there.

'Oh. Where did you pop up from?' Then she gasped, realising how rude that sounded. 'Sorry. I didn't hear you. I am supposed to be at the bank by now, but …' Margot didn't really want to say how she'd felt earlier. 'I decided to take another day off.' she finished lamely.

'Understandable.' Bessie nodded. Her eyes seemed to penetrate Margot's to the very depth of her soul, but she said no more.

Feeling she should explain further, although she didn't know why, she told Bessie how she'd thought it would be nice to take a look inside the church.

'But it's locked up. I'll come another day, a bit later, in the afternoon, maybe.' She knew she was rambling, and took a deep breath. 'Now I'm here, I thought it would be a nice idea to try and find Meg and Miles' graves. That's if they are buried here, of course. If they are, perhaps I could tidy their graves up?'

Bessie nodded. 'That's a nice idea. I's doubting many people even know about her.' She looked beyond Margot's shoulders and pointed to a spot. 'Mistress Meg is just there,' she said, pointing to the grave. 'And Lord Miles is buried beside her.'

Margot turned around to see where Bessie was pointing, and moved slowly towards them. Bessie stood back and watched. The nearer Margot got, the harder she found it to breathe and walk, with her feet

The Return

dragging heavily as she forced herself along.

   I don't think I can do this.

7

Margot stopped. Unable to move, she concentrated on the back of the two graves. She knew she would have to take a look, even if it was just to confirm Meg was actually buried there.

So, why have I got this creepy feeling ... one of them belongs to me? For goodness sake, now I'm being ridiculous, I'm here, and I'm alive ... aren't I? Just to prove it, Margot pinched her arm. *Yes, I'm definitely alive.*

She looked over her shoulder to see if Bessie was still there. She was, and quietly watching her. Margot gave a weak smile. 'It feels as if I'm intruding, that I shouldn't be here. At the same time, I know I have to read the epitaph.'

Bessie moved up and stood beside her. 'I's with

The Return

you if'n you need me. Take your time.'

They both stood lost in their own world, Bessie's face giving away nothing, whilst Margot's indecision was as clear as if it had been tattooed on her forehead.

I can't do this. I really don't want to do this.

'Which one of them is Miles' resting place?' Margot asked, knowing she was only putting off the moment. But it might give her the push she needed.

'That one,' Bessie pointed to the grave that was so close to Megs, it was almost touching.'He were determined to lay next to her until…' She coughed. 'I's sorry, but I've got a tickle in the back of my throat,' she said, adding another cough as if to prove it. She continued coughing until she saw Margot move over to Miles' grave.

Bessie gave an occasional cough whenever Margot looked back at her. Then, what she'd been hoping for finally happened. Margot was kneeling beside Miles' headstone, rubbing away the lichen to see his name.

'You'd think the church would tend the graves of those who no longer have family to do it, wouldn't you?' Margot remarked as she continued pulling off the lichen. Once the letters were legible, she looked closer at the dates. 'It says he was born on the twelve of July 1850, and died on the twentieth of January 1940. He was nearly ninety years old. He lived to a great old age.'

'Yes, he did. They weren't happy years, though.

He never got over losing Mistress Meg.'

But you were worth waiting for, my sweet Meg

.   The words seemed to float in the air, then gently move like a caress through Margot's mind. Margot pulled herself up and looked around. 'He's here.' She turned to Bessie. 'But you knew that, didn't you?'

Bessie kept quiet. Waiting and watching,

'You want me to go to Meg's grave now, don't you? Well, I'm not. I want to know what the hell is going on before I do that.' She glared at Bessie with defiant, challenging eyes.

Not receiving any comments, Margot turned on her heel and walked away with Bessie chasing after her.

'I's don't know much more'n you do,' she said. 'I just know you belong together.'

Margot spun around furiously. 'He's *dead*, Bessie. And if you hadn't noticed, I'm *alive*. What do you want me to do … *kill* myself?'

'No. Course I don't.' Bessie shifted her focus to the ground, not able to look Margot in the eyes.

'Look, Bessie, I am not Meg. As much as you and Miles' ghost might like to think I am, I am not.' With that, Margot turned and ran off, leaving a forlorn Bessie staring after her.

Back at the house, Margot managed to regain control of her emotions. Then, without the faintest idea why, she went up to the attic.

The Return

'This has got to be where the answers are,' she muttered. 'But first, I have to understand the questions.' Her eyes moved over the trunks and stopped at the one containing the wedding gown. Lifting the lid, she pulled the dress out and held it up.

It's stunning. What a shame you didn't get to wear it. She gently replaced it, then opened the trunk beside it. There was a dress at the top.

'I don't remember seeing this one last time.' She picked it up and held it out to get a better look. It was a beautiful emerald green, with a sequined bodice, and short puffed sleeves with a lace trim. It was obviously a ball gown.

Just like the time she first held the wedding dress; she saw herself dressed in the exquisite gown. Music was playing, Margot closed her eyes as she listened to the sounds that floated around her. Then she was being swept around the ballroom, dancing the waltz, laughing up into his face, Miles' face. Oh, how handsome he was. Her heart was full to bursting with love for him. She wanted it to be like this forever. To stay in his arms.

'I was right. The green matches the colour of your emerald eyes, perfectly,' he whispered into her hair, his smile captured in the warmth of his voice. 'And those sequins make them sparkle like diamonds in starlight. You are so beautiful, my sweet Meg. Please come back to me...' His voice faded as the music drifted away leaving Margot alone in the attic again. Her heart ached; tears slid softly over her cheeks.

'Oh.' The dress slipped from Margot's grasp. 'What just happened?' She wiped her hand over her wet cheeks, still painfully aware of the emptiness inside her heart.

She sat down on the nearest trunk and picked up the dress. Holding it close, she tried to recall his face. It was a blur, but she had seen it, and she remembered thinking he was so handsome.

Margot stood up and, still holding the dress, she raced down to her bedroom. Stripping off her clothes, she stood in front of the full-length mirror and stepped into the gown. She couldn't reach to do up all the tiny pearl buttons at the back, so held it together with one hand and stared at her reflection.

'Oh, Mistress Meg.' Bessie came over and did up the little buttons. 'I's knew it was you.'

That Margot hadn't heard her coming up the stairs didn't surprise her at all. She realised this was going to keep happening, and in that moment, she made her decision.

'Bessie. I don't know exactly what you are, or where you came from. You could be a ghost, or someone who has discovered the secret of immortality, but I do know you have something to do with what's been happening; so how about you start talking. If you want my help, I need to know

The Return

everything you know. I have to be prepared for whatever will happen when I go and see Meg's grave.'

Bessie sucked in her bottom lip and held it tight with her teeth. Her eyes glazed over as she appeared to think about it. 'Can we talk over a cup of that nice coffee?'

Margot rolled her eyes and laughed. 'Okay. Help me out of this and I'll put my own clothes back on.'

The buttons were the fiddliest, but Bessie soon had them undone and helped Margot step out of the gown. 'I think I'll keep it down here,' Margot said, draping it over her arm. 'I'll use one of the spare bedrooms to put it in for now.'

'I'll go and put the kettle on,' Bessie told her. She'd soon learned how to make a pot of coffee, and the packets of tea had been relegated to the back of the cupboard. By the time Margot joined her in the kitchen, Bessie had everything ready.

'So, tell me all you know about what happened to Miles after Meg's death,' Margot said, after the coffee was poured. 'Oh, do you fancy a biscuit with it? I've got some nice digestive dunkers.' Before Bessie could answer, Margot was bringing the biscuit tin to the table.

'Dunkers? What's them?'

Margot opened the tin and took out one of the plain biscuits. 'These,' she said, dipping the biscuit into the coffee before eating it. 'It's lovely, try it.'

'I's gonna take your word for it,' she smiled. 'I's liking my coffee as it is.' She took a sip and almost purred. 'Now, let's see. What was Miles like after Mistress Meg's death? Broken, in a word. He never recovered. She were the only woman he ever loved.'

'Didn't he ever find someone he could be happy with?'

'He never looked. He never went to the society parties to meet anyone. In fact, he became more of a recluse. It were sad. His father kept on at him to get married and give him an heir. Sometimes I's thinking it were Miles' way of getting his own back on his Lordship.'

'What happened to the estate after Miles died? Was there another cousin ... someone who would inherit it?'

'Well, that's the thing. He didn't leave it to no one. He had a friend who were a solicitor and said he were to take the money from the estate and invest it. But he said they had to use some to take care of the house until such a day came when a person would come to claim it.

'He gave his friend two letters and said they must be passed down to each consecutive solicitor. One letter was addressed to the solicitor of the day, so he would know what to do with the second letter. That letter was to remain unopened and given to the

The Return

claimant.'

Margot thought about that; it did make sense. 'And you know all this because...?'

Bess shrugged. 'I just do.'

Did I really expect a proper answer? 'What I can't understand is, Meg is dead and so is Miles. Why didn't he go and join her? Why is he hanging around down here?'

There was a rather lengthy silence as Margot waited for Bessie's answer.

'He's been waiting for you to come back to him.'

8

How did I know you were going to say that?' Margot hadn't been shocked. What with all that had been going on, she was slowly coming around to acknowledging she *might be* the Meg who had lived in a previous time. She certainly was according to Miles and Bessie. But there was still a niggle at the back of her mind.

'Okay, just supposing that what you're saying, combined with what's been happening to me, is true, that I *am* the reincarnation of Meg. What happens to me, in the here and now, if I am taken back in time? I was born and brought up here, I can't just *not* exist. What about all the things I've done? Surely, I've left my footprint somewhere? Perhaps I've made a difference to someone's life? I'd like to think I have,

The Return

anyway.' Margot paused and looked thoughtful.

'I suppose it's possible that my life has been so hum-drum I could be deleted and no one would know I'd ever existed. I don't think I like that idea.'

'I's imagine that'll all have been sorted. I's going to tell you something else that's been on my mind.' Bessie patted Margot's arm. 'I's had this feeling Mistress Meg weren't supposed to die when she did, and you … you've gotta put it right.'

They were silent for a few minutes and then Margot started laughing. 'Listen to us. Anyone would think it was just a case of me hailing a taxi and asking the driver to take me back to 1886. How on earth am I going to put it right when it happened over a hundred years ago?'

'I's thinking you must go to Mistress Meg's grave. I's not knowing that for sure, mind, but that seems to be where you're being directed.'

'Mmm. Although I can't see what visiting someone's grave is going to do, I do know I have to go there.' She picked up her coffee and took a sip. 'I've got to phone my manager and tell him I need a few more days off, just in case we find there is such a thing as a time-travelling taxi.' She laughed, then took another sip before putting her cup down. 'I'll do it now, while I think of it.'

For the next few hours, Bessie stayed to help Margot go through the remaining unopened trunks.

Those containing clothes were emptied and taken down to join the emerald green ball gown. The room soon took on the appearance of a period costume department for Hollywood movies. Some didn't look to be worth keeping, but most were in immaculate condition.

The final trunk was filled with a wide selection of shoes and boots, all of which fitted Margot perfectly. Not that she fancied wearing them in public as some were quite ugly, and uncomfortable.

'I'm sure our local museum would love to get their hands on these. They'd be quite a draw, especially because they once belonged to a local woman. But I'll sort that out later.' Margot looked at her watch. 'Crikey, look at the time. No wonder I'm hungry. What about you?'

Bessie was holding up an open gold locket. She turned it to show Margot the two pictures inside. 'This is Mistress Meg and this one is Miles.'

Margot stared at the locket, then opened her hand so Bessie could lay it in her palm. 'You'n Meg could be twins,' she said, watching Margot's eyes widen with surprise.

There was no getting away from it. If Margot didn't know better, she would think it was a photo of her. 'It's uncanny.' She looked at the picture of Miles, and gasped. 'He's just as I saw him in my vision. I couldn't remember how he looked once he'd

The Return

disappeared, but this is definitely him. He's rather handsome, isn't he?'

'Yes, he were a looker, all right.' Bessie sighed, but a little smile lifted her lips. 'And she were a beauty, too.'

'Their eyes … they both look so sad.'

'Mmm, they would be. These were taken by the photographer who was booked for the wedding pictures. I's thinking Miles sorted that out, him being a friend'n all.'

Whatever doubts Margot might have had were now completely wiped away. Seeing those photos had convinced her. She handed the locket back to Bessie. 'If I can help them, then I will. I don't know how this will work, but if Miles has somehow worked it out, I'll do it.'

'You won't regret it.' Bessie was beyond excited. 'We'll go to the church tomorrow and I's going to be with you all the way, of course.'

'That's a relief. Now that's been decided, I'll leave all these lovely dresses here for now, and take them to the museum when I come back. … I've decided to go with the idea that I will be coming back because if we do stop Meg's death happening ... well, I wouldn't be needed, would I?' She looked at Bessie with raised eyebrows and her head tilted sideways. But before she could reply, Margot answered her own question. 'Of course, I wouldn't. Come on, let's go and find something to eat.'

****

The following morning, Margot woke with a sense of anticipation she hadn't felt in a long time. There was also a feeling of trepidation due to the unknown, but she quickly shoved that aside. Today her questions should get answered. Would she get to meet Miles in the flesh? That thought made her heart flutter. She took a deep breath and climbed out of bed.

Bessie was already sitting at the kitchen table, nursing a cup of coffee, when Margot walked in. Smelling the coffee, she made straight for the cooking range where the pot was being kept piping hot, and poured herself a cup.

'Good morning, did you sleep well?' Margot asked as she took some bread from the bin and cut two thick slices off to toast.

'I's slept good. What about you? You look as bright as a button,' Bessie replied, putting her cup back on the table.

'Yes, I do feel good. Now I've decided to help Meg and Miles, I can't wait to get on with it. Shall I cut you a slice?' Margot asked.

'No, I's had mine, thanks.'

'Right, tell me how you think this is going to work,' Margot said, once her toast was ready and she was sitting, spreading it with butter and thick-cut

The Return

marmalade.

'I's don't rightly know. But we both know it has something to do with Meg's grave. I's thinking you will know when you touch it.'

'Mmm, that's what I think, too. Yesterday, as I moved closer to it, I had a strange feeling of being pulled. Quite creepy, I can tell you.' She filled her mouth with the last of the toast, then wiped her mouth with a piece of kitchen roll.

Bessie stood up and took her cup over to the sink, hesitated, then turned to the coffee pot. 'I's not knowing if I'll be getting another cup of this,' she said, pouring the coffee.

Margot's eyebrows shot up at that, but she kept quiet. *Perhaps she meant, when she'd get another cup of coffee, not, if she would.*

Once Margot had cleared away the breakfast things, she went to her room and finished getting ready. Just as she was slipping on her shoes, an unexpected bout of nerves seized her, causing her to grab hold of the bedpost and take some long deep breaths until it passed.

'You can do this, Margot. Don't back out now.' She stared at herself in the mirror. 'So, tell me, will I be Margot or Meg next time I stand in this room?' Her reflection stared back with glazed eyes. 'Hmm, a lot of good you are.'

'I see you're ready and raring to go.' Margot

grinned as she came down the stairs and saw Bessie standing by the door. 'Okay. Let's get off.'

Whether it was due to nerves or they'd both run out of something to say, neither of them spoke until they'd walked up the road and arrived at the church.

Margot tried the door, and was pleased to find it open. 'I think I'd like to go inside for a few minutes.' Margot said softly. 'It would be nice to have God on our side before we do whatever it is we'll be doing.' Bessie nodded and followed her in.

It was a small church, but beautiful and so peaceful. Margot closed her eyes, breathing in the aroma of oak pews and candle wax.

It's strange how there's a distinct scent that belongs to all churches.

Moving up the aisle, they slipped into one of the pews and knelt on the prayer cushions. With her hands clasped, and her elbows resting on the back of the bench in front of her, Margot stared at the lovely stained-glass window that showed Mary holding the baby Jesus in her arms. She could almost feel the love that flowed between them.

Dear God, please guide me through the journey I have to make. Help me do the right thing. I don't know what to expect, but I do know it feels right.

She turned to face the statue of Jesus on the cross. His eyes seemed to stare directly into hers and held

The Return

for a moment until Margot's dropped. A feeling so powerful spread through her and she knew, without a doubt, that what she was about to do was with His blessing.

'Are you ready to go, Bessie?' she whispered. Receiving just a nod, Margot stood up and they both left the church. The sun was shining, even though there was a slight nip in the air.

Bessie led the way through the cemetery, stopping at the two graves belonging to Meg and Miles. She stared at them for a moment before looking up at Margot. The unspoken question was clearly defined on her face. Without a word, Margot knelt beside Meg's grave and read the inscription.

28-10-1857 - 11-11-1886

My sweet Meg

I will wait forever for your return

Throwing one last glance at Bessie, Margot took a deep breath and, hesitating for only a heartbeat, she lifted her hand and touched the headstone....

9

Margot's fingertips barely grazed the top of Meg's headstone when she felt a tingling sensation travel up her arm. She tried to pull away as it continued over her body, but a hidden force held her hand captive.

Although Margot had mentally prepared herself for something strange to happen, it wasn't enough to stop the overwhelming fear which enveloped her when the sky plunged into absolute darkness; as if the sun's fiery luminosity had been snuffed out in an instant.

'Bessie? Are you there?' On hearing her quivering voice sound more alien than human, Margot's nerves plummeted. Her breathing came in short bursts, and her heartbeat raced more like a drum roll than the

The Return

steady tick-tock of a clock.

Margot tried to take a deep breath to calm herself, but it stuck in her throat; panic had taken hold like an iron fist squeezing the life out of her. Just when she thought her heart would explode, a violent pressure hit her body, sending her careering forward to land face down on the ground.

Holding her breath, she remained there, trying to keep as still as the corpses buried around her. Margot kept her eyes squeezed shut. She didn't dare lift her lids, not even a little. Finally, when nothing else happened, she found the courage to take a look. From her prone position, she raised her head a fraction—it all looked normal.

She closed her eyes again, just for a moment, allowing the warm feeling of immense relief to flood through her, replacing the icy fingers of fear. With slow, unsteady movements, Margot managed to get to her feet.

The first major change she noticed was Meg's and Miles' headstones had disappeared. Turning around, she saw the cemetery was empty apart from two people, one standing and one kneeling beside a freshly filled grave.

'The new grave is Lady Emma Crawford's, the one beside it is her husband's, and those people are Lady Margaret, you know as Meg, and Lord Miles Brandon.'

Sandra Stoner-Mitchell

Margot spun round. 'Bessie. Oh, Bessie, you have no idea how pleased I am to see you, but how come you're here? Did you touch Meg's headstone, too?'

Bessie's eyes twinkled with merriment as she replied, 'I's didn't need to, my dear. I's not from your time, or this time—I's belonging to all time.'

Margot's jaw dropped as her eyes widened with bemusement. She shook her head, deciding not to bother asking for an explanation, that could wait; she was confused enough already.

'Okay. We're both here. I'm assuming this is 1886?'

'Mmm. October 1886. Yours and Mistress Meg's birthdays are coming up soon and Meg'll die two-weeks later … You's gotta stop that from happening.'

'But how can I do that? What will people say if they see two Megs?' She looked down at the clothes she'd put on that morning. 'Though, they might be more interested in what I'm wearing rather than me. I doubt my jeans, baggy jumper, and leather jacket are the fashion of the day.'

'No one can see you but me. So don't you go fretting about that.' Bessie smiled, and laid her hand on Margot's arm. 'We's wanting to find out what caused Mistress Meg's fall from her horse. Who messed with her saddle? And why? Once we knows that, you can start your job.'

'Oh, is that all?' Margot retorted. But her caustic

The Return

remark bounced off Bessie. She rolled her eyes and sighed. 'Okay, where shall we start?'

'That's a good question. Perhaps it'll be best if we just watch and listen for a day or two. I's wondering if'n we visit Mistress Meg's brother tomorrow we might learn something that'll give us a bit of a clue.'

'That's a good idea, considering you believe he told Miles' father where Meg lived, and that Miles had continued seeing her.'

'Exactly. For now, let's go over and listen to what's going on with Miles and Mistress Meg.'

*****

Meg shifted her weight as she knelt beside her father's grave. For the first time since his suicide, she could allow the tears to flow freely and grieve the loss of the man he was before his gambling had destroyed all their lives. Eight years was a long time to keep the resentment simmering. Forgiving him allowed her to remember the happy times they'd shared.

She looked over at her mother's fresh grave, and gave a tremulous smile. Lady Crawford had insisted, long before she died, that she be laid to rest next to her beloved husband in the unconsecrated area reserved for those who died by their own hand, along with the unbaptised. Her refusal to believe that the God she loved would not forgive him, had angered the vicar, but she wouldn't be swayed.

'Perhaps now you're together again, you'll both find peace. I do sincerely hope so; and I pray God has welcomed you both home.' Standing up, Meg waited for the pins and needles in her legs to let up before she turned and smiled at Miles.

'Thank you for coming with me,' she said softly.

He was beside her in an instant and, wrapping his arms around her, he buried his face in her fiery red hair. Then, with his hands on her shoulders, he held her away so she could look up into his eyes.

'I'll always be with you, my sweet Meg, never forget that.' He let his lips brush hers and then, pulling her close, he looked over her head and stared straight into Margot's eyes and smiled. 'Until time ceases and infinity has been breached, I will be with you. You already know that, don't you?'

*****

Margot shivered, and wrapped her arms around herself. 'Did you see that, Bessie?' her voice, no more than a whisper, while her eyes watched Miles turn and walk away with Meg. 'He saw me. He looked straight into my eyes and, not only that, I'm sure he was speaking to me. I thought you said no one could see me?'

Bessie nodded. 'No one else can, but you knew Miles could, Margot. You told me yourself that he came to you. Why are you surprised that he can see

The Return

you now?'

'I know, but I thought that was just because he was looking for Meg, this Meg, the one who died.' Margot said, genuinely at a loss now. 'Does he want both of us?' This was something she'd not anticipated, and quite frankly, wasn't sure she liked, either.

'I's thinking you're making too much of this,' Bessie said calmly. 'So, before you let your imagination run away with you any further, remember what you're here for. It's your job to find out what happened to Mistress Meg, and then you can right this wrong.'

Margot smiled. 'Thanks, I needed that. What do we do now? Miles has taken Meg back home. Should we follow?'

'That's a good idea. You needs to learn more about Mistress Meg, and listening in can help a lot.'

*****

Back at the house that Miles had bought for her and her mother all those years ago, it seemed so empty with just her there, alone, now that her mother had died. Meg could feel the tears filling her eyes, and blinked them away. She didn't want Miles to see; he worried enough about her already.

She watched as he poured them both a drink. *If only we could be married, I'd never be alone again.*

'Here, this will warm you up,' Miles said, handing

her a small glass of brandy. He raised his own glass, and smiled. 'Here's to your mother–may she at last find happiness now that she's with your father.'

Meg gave a feeble smile, raised her glass and took a sip. She let the warm, smooth liquid do its work before moving over to sit beside the fire. She couldn't remember ever being truly happy, not since that day...

'Miles? What do I do now? I don't have any friends; your father has seen to that. I don't have you really. So, what is the point of it all?'

The pain that crossed Miles' face made Meg feel guilty. 'Oh, Miles, I'm sorry. There's me just thinking of myself, while you ... What a selfish fool I am.'

In an instant, Miles was on his knees in front of her. He took the glass from her and put it on the hearth. His eyes searching hers as he took both her hands in his. 'Never, ever think that, my sweet Meg. You are my life, my heart, you are the air I breathe. Soon, my love, soon we'll be together all the time. I'm going to speak to my father tonight.'

Meg gasped. 'No Miles. You mustn't do that. It might make matters worse. I'm sorry I mentioned it now; it's just me wallowing in self-pity. I'm all right, truly I am. I think it's because my mother is no longer here for me to care for and talk to. I miss her already. But give me a little time and I'll be fine. Just knowing you love me is enough.'

The Return

Miles' face was dark with anger. 'Society and their arrogance. My damned father being the worst of the lot. Sometimes, I wish that it was him who'd died. He hasn't an ounce of love in his heart for anyone but himself. At least I could have helped your father, and we'd be married.' He brought her hands up to his lips and kissed each of her fingers.

'You mustn't say such things, Miles. We will get married; I feel sure of it.' Meg said, sounding more confident than she felt.

Miles stood and looked into Meg's upturned face. 'I'm just going to check if my horse has been stabled for the night, and then I'll be back. I'm staying tonight.'

He walked over to the door and turned. Looking straight at Margot, he gave a barely discernible flick of his head, then walked out.

10

Margot and Bessie stopped a few yards away while Miles went in and spoke to the stable hand. On his way out, he signalled for them to follow.

They caught up with him around the side of the house and an instant spark ignited between Margot and Miles as they stared into each other's eyes.

'Hello, Meg.' His soft, provocative voice was more like a caress; seductive, yet gently teasing.

Not a good start. Margot wrestled with her bedroom thoughts, dispatching them quickly to the back of her mind. *Miles, as an amorous ghost, had been bad enough, but to handle the living, breathing, magnificent hunk of a man in real life ... that would be too much to cope with.*

The Return

He took her hand and held it to his lips, stirring exquisite, sensual feelings right to the core of her being. She tried so hard, albeit unsuccessfully, to fight against them.

This is getting worse by the second.

'At last, we meet in my time. It's been my pleasure knowing you in the future.' He gave a rascally grin, keeping a firm hold of her hand.

Now you've gone too far.

'Well, it certainly wasn't *my* pleasure.' she retorted, not wanting him to think she'd enjoyed it too. But it was obvious she'd failed—miserably. His raised eyebrow and the curl of his lips, told her so.

'Let's get two things straight, your *Lordship*, first, I am *not* your Meg, I'm Margot,' she snapped, blushing scarlet. 'And … and secondly, I'm not here to accommodate your frustrated carnal desires. I'm here to help Meg and, if I'm not mistaken, that's why you had me come here, isn't it?' she finished, quite flustered.

Miles stared at her for a long moment before replying. 'You're absolutely right, of course. It's just that when I'm with you, you *are* Meg. I've never seen a more remarkable likeness, not only in looks, but also in the kind-hearted, warm, and loving nature the pair of you share. Please, will you accept my sincere apology?'

Margot studied his firm, square jaw, not wanting

to look into his pleading eyes. She knew she'd forgive him. She also knew there was nothing really to forgive him for, but she wasn't going to let him know that.

She had no choice. She had to look up into those coal-black eyes that bore into hers. Her lips parted allowing her rapid breathing to escape.

But it was the emotions overtaking her that were the problem. They were the most scandalous, but incredibly breath-taking feelings of raw passion she had ever felt. She was discovering, to her dismay, how easy it would be to fall in love with him. Not only that, she knew she'd find it hard to go back to her own time without him.

Margot realised she'd be lost if she didn't pull away; moreso when her fingers began twitching, desperately wanting to run amok in his long, soft, wavy hair. It was only then she managed to jerk her hand from his and move—just a small step away.

There should be a law against men like Miles walking around, oozing such incredible sex appeal.

She took a deep breath, 'Of course, I accept your apology, and I appreciate it.' She surprised herself at how calm she sounded, and couldn't control the wide smile that glued itself to her face when she watched him visibly relax and release a sigh of relief.

'You must have found it terrifying travelling

The Return

back to my century and coming face to face with yourself,' he said, changing the subject. 'When I saw you in the future ... Well, let's just say I understand just how you must feel.'

'It was rather frightening, I have to admit,' Margot replied. 'At least when I travel back, I'll know what to expect. You must have found it disconcerting, too.'

'Yes, I must have.' He frowned and shook his head. He gave Margot a strange look, as if he'd only just seen her. 'I went to the future, to find you ... didn't I?' He rubbed his forehead, not expecting a reply. 'I'm well aware of the reason you're here ... It has to do with Meg ... I think something terrible is going to happen to her.' He stopped, his frown deepening. 'Unfortunately, it's all rather vague.'

Margot waited, now as confused as Miles sounded, and wondered if a gentle nudge to remind him of Meg's impending death, would help; but decided against it after glancing over at Bessie's usual impassive, unhelpful expression.

'I seem to remember someone opening a portal into the future so I could go through and find you.' Miles pushed an errant lock of his hair back from his eyes, and stared blindly into the distance. 'I just can't remember why. How could I have forgotten something as important as that?'

Miles leaned back against the brick wall of the

house, putting his hands in his pocket, then taking them out again. 'I know I need you to help me stop whatever it was from taking place. One thing I am sure of is, my father will be involved. How? I haven't the faintest idea.' The more he spoke, the more frustrated and befuddled he became. 'I just know I have to save Meg.'

From the hard, fierce expression in his eyes, Margot could tell his unwavering love for Meg could not be challenged. It was absolute.

'That's what we're here to do. Bessie has some ideas that we are going to look into tomorrow.'

Miles immediately recovered from his musings at the mention of Bessie, and his smile returned. 'Hello, Bessie. You will have to forgive me, but although I'm sure we've met before, my mind seems to have buried itself in a fog. Was it you who helped me through the portal?'

Bessie nodded, and he continued, 'It was also you who helped convince Margot to come back with you, wasn't it?'

'Yes, it was. But don't worry about your memory. Travelling through time takes a lot of energy, but you'll be as right as rain shortly,' Bessie told him, patting his arm. 'Margot and I's here to find out what happened, and then stop it. If you can remember anything, no matter how small, it might be a good idea if you could tell us now.'

The Return

Miles nodded and looked at the ground, appearing distracted. He rubbed his hand over his chin and frowned. 'As I've already said, I think my father is behind it. I don't know why I think that, but it's in my head and I can't shift it. As far as he's concerned, Meg is the one person standing in my way of marrying and producing an heir. What he doesn't realise is, I won't marry anyone but Meg.'

He paused and closed his eyes. When he opened them, they were clear and focused. 'Richard. Meg's brother. He's bound to be involved, as well.'

'That's good, Miles. We can work on that. Thank you.' Bessie smiled. Although they hadn't learned much more than they already knew, it wouldn't help any of them to say so.

*****

After Miles left them, Margot turned to Bessie, a frown puckering her forehead. 'What happened? The longer he was with us, the more his memory failed him. He was fine to start with. How is that possible?'

'It won't be long before he forgets it all, and he won't be able to see us, either. He can't be allowed to remember what he learned in the future. It might not be much, but the results would be catastrophic in your time.' Bessie sighed and pursed her lips. 'It would've been so different if'n I'd been here when all this happened, but I's were sent to help out elsewhere.'

'At least Miles has confirmed your suspicions about Meg's brother. Do you know where he lives?'

Bessie nodded. 'Yes, let's make our way over there now. We can have a browse around once he goes to bed.'

*****

Miles did stay the night just as he'd promised, cradling Meg in his arms until she fell asleep. His thoughts were all over the place remembering what she'd said.

She's right, she has no friends now. The ones she had, even her best friend, were all forbidden to see her by their own parents. Mostly because they didn't want to upset my father. If only Lord Crawford had come to me, all this could have been avoided.

Lying in bed unable to sleep, Miles thought of Meg's upcoming birthday the following week. He'd already decided on her present and couldn't wait to give it to her.

I'll never forgive you for what you've done, Father. You want me to get married to some woman I don't know or love, and give you another heir to keep the family line going? Huh, you'll not have one from me. Not now, not ever.

It had crossed his mind a few times that Meg and

The Return

he hadn't already produced a child. Their lovemaking was never anything less than unrestrained ecstasy. She was a remarkable and affectionate, sweet woman, who loved him as much as he loved her, but there was no pregnancy. *That will serve him right.*

As Meg lay in his arms, he allowed himself to luxuriate in her delicious scent, and, holding her closer, he listened to the soft rhythm of her breathing as she slept. In that instant, he made his decision.

Nothing and no one will stop me. I will marry Meg, even if it means we have to move away from here.

Miles lay there trying to work things out. It would need careful planning and he couldn't tell Meg. *A Christmas wedding.* Miles fell asleep with a smile on his face.

Sandra Stoner-Mitchell

11

Richard's house was at the end of a long, curved, private road, surrounded by woodlands and beautiful well-tended gardens. It wasn't quite what Margot had been expecting considering he'd lost out on his inheritance. A property boasting such impressive grandeur had to belong to someone who not only had the money to buy it, but also to maintain it.

There was no time to question Bessie; she was marching ahead with the vitality of a woman half her age. Margot was hard pressed to keep up. It was a long walk around to the side of the mansion, where Bessie led the way down some steps. The door at the bottom, leading into the kitchen, was unlocked.

Of the three women in the kitchen, two were busy

The Return

sorting out trays of meat, and the third, a teenage girl, was hard at work scrubbing down the large wooden table.

All three looked up expectantly when the door opened. Not able to see Bessie and Margot as they walked in, the women looked at each other with expressions revealing their uncertainty.

'How'd that happen?' The older woman's face screwed up, her eyes squinting, as she stared at the open door. 'There ain't so much as a breeze about.'

She rubbed her hands down her apron front before walking over and taking a look outside. Seeing no one on the steps, she came back in and closed the door, shaking the handle to make sure it was shut fast.

She walked back to where she'd been working, aware of the expectant looks of the other two. 'Bleedin' kids messin' around again,' she said angrily. 'If I gets me 'ands on 'em, I'll give 'em wot for, you mark my words.'

Bessie looked at Margot and grinned. 'This is the fun part of being invisible. But we's have to be careful not to knock into anything. We's don't want them thinking there's ghosts about.'

The thought of that made Margot laugh.

Moving out of the kitchen, Margot was amazed at the richness of her surroundings; it was stunning. The central elegant stairway, leading off at the top in two directions, had Margot mesmerised. She'd never seen anything as grand.

'I thought Richard was penniless. How can he afford a place like this?' Margot whispered.

Bessie looked around and shrugged. 'It's okay if'n you like this type of thing. How Richard ended up here was pure chance. His father-in-law, Mr Turnbull, who just happened to be very rich, persuaded him to marry his daughter after finding out that Richard would keep his title of Lord. When Lady Gwendolyn's father died a year later, they inherited all this and more.'

'Why on earth would Mr Turnbull do that?'

'When you sees Lady Gwendolyn, you'll understand. She's not the prettiest flower in the garden, or the brightest light in the chandelier. I's thinking she's happy enough in her own way, and she's produced Richard a son and heir. I spose that's one of Richard's many reasons why he rarely stays here now; he's got the money, he's got the estate, and he's got an heir,' Bessie said, unable to keep the disgust out of her voice.

'Nowadays, he much prefers to spend his time in London with his mistress. But unfortunately, he's here now, meaning we'll have to wait for a while before we can go rummaging around in his study searching for clues.'

'How awful. Does Gwendolyn know about the mistress?'

The Return

'Course she does. She doesn't care; it keeps him out of her bed.'

'What an awful life she must have. I wouldn't want my husband sleeping around.' The mere idea of it turned Margot's stomach.

Bessie smiled, but said nothing.

'What I still don't understand is why would Richard go and tell Miles' father about Meg still seeing his son? He has what he wants now. Why ruin it for Meg?'

'I's thinking it's because his sister will have more status than he would. Miles' dad is a Duke, see, and when he dies, Miles will take the title, and his wife would become a Duchess. He would have to call them His Grace and Her Grace. I's don't think he'd be liking that.'

'So he'd ruin her life because of a title? How disgusting. I didn't like him before, and I like him even less now. And I've never met the man.'

The sound of voices coming from the grand curved stairway had them look up and watch as two people came down.

'That's Richard and Gwendolyn,' Bessie said, sniffing disdainfully. 'He gets right up my nose.'

Gwendolyn certainly wasn't born with any pleasing features, in fact, Margot felt quite sorry for her. Not because she was beyond plain, but that everyone, including her father, had thought of her that way. They hadn't bothered to get to know the woman beneath the looks. Surely, she had some pleasant attributes?

As soon as Richard was standing in the reception area, a butler came through with his coat, hat and gloves.

'I've sent for your carriage, Sir, it will be here by the time you're ready.' He helped Richard on with his coat, and handed him the hat and gloves. By the time the butler had opened the door, Richard's carriage was there waiting.

'I will see you in the morning, my dear. Don't wait up.' Richard gave her the required peck on her cheek, then turned and left before she could answer.

Gwendolyn stared at the closed door with hate-filled eyes as she used her lace handkerchief to scrub her cheek where Richard's lips had touched. When she'd finished, she handed the soiled cloth to the butler.

'Please dispose of this, Jenkins.'

'Yes, my lady. Will there be anything else? Some refreshment?'

'That's very thoughtful of you, Jenkins, but perhaps I'll indulge myself with something a little stronger tonight.' When Jenkins started to move towards her sitting room, Gwendolyn raised her hand. 'Don't worry, I'll pour my own. You can go off for the night now.'

The Return

'Very good, my lady.'

She turned and left him. Jenkins watched her until she disappeared, a sympathetic look spreading across his face before he hurried off.

Bessie and Margot had watched and listened, fascinated. 'So much for you thinking she was happy enough,' Margot said sadly. 'She can't stand the man, and, quite frankly, I don't blame her.'

'Mmm. Yes, that was a surprise. I's thinking we'll have to watch her.' Bessie scratched her head, then patting Margot on the arm, said, 'Come on, let's check out his private study and see if we can find anything interesting.'

The first thing Margot noticed when they walked into the room was the distinct lack of anything relating to Richard personally. Most of the features were of the previous owner, Gwendolyn's father.

'It doesn't look as if he spends much time in here,' she said, opening and
closing drawers and cupboards. 'There's nothing here that would be useful to us.'

'No.' Bessie sat in the large mahogany and leather desk chair. 'I's thinking it might be better to look more into our Lady Gwendolyn. She's the one that'll be carrying the grudge.'

'Against Meg? Why?'

'No, not against Meg, but through her. Gwendolyn knows how much Richard hates his sister. Now, what if she finds out there's a party coming up for Meg's birthday. Don't you think that would give her great pleasure telling Richard that Miles is still with Meg? I's thinking how outraged that would make him? Especially if it comes from his *beloved* wife.'

Margot thought for a moment. 'That would put the cat amongst the pigeons, wouldn't it? So how would we stop her … if it is her that starts it off?'

'I's not been thinking that far yet, and I might be way off. We's got to keep our options open. I's thinking we should go and give Miles' father's house a visit tomorrow. He's the one that'll blow his top when he finds out what's been going on.'

'Yes, I'd very much like to meet this dreadful man and give him a piece of my mind.'

'Well, you can't be doing that.' Bessie chortled. 'Let's go and keep Gwendolyn company.'

The Return

12

Alone at last, Gwendolyn headed straight for the drinks cabinet and picked up the decanted malt whisky. She poured a small amount into a glass, taking a moment to appreciate the aroma and enjoy the tingling sensation on the roof of her mouth. Then, tipping the glass to her lips she let the whisky coat her tongue before swallowing. The warm burn that followed was the most satisfying of all. She sighed and, for the tiniest fraction of time, she felt content.

When her eyes glanced up to the portrait of her father and his dark, soulless eyes stared back, Gwendolyn's thin lips pinched into a tight smile of contempt. 'Why I keep you up there, I don't know. One of these days, I'll throw you on the fire, and sit there while you warm my feet.'

She took another sip of whisky, a larger one this time, as her disgruntled mood returned. The portrait had always frightened her when she was younger. It was his eyes. Wherever she was in the room, those blistering orbs would be looking straight at her. There was no escape.

She looked away and walked over to the portrait of herself sitting on the chair, with Richard standing behind her with that pompous look on his face. 'You'll soon be going on the fire, too.' Gwendolyn laughed, not unlike an old washer-woman's harsh cackle, and took a larger swig of whisky.

With a sudden mood swing, she snatched the hem of her long skirt and started dancing around the room. With her glass still clutched in her other hand, she held her arm out, curving it, as she would if dancing with a partner.

Her laughter turned manic, and throwing her head back, she spun faster, letting her full skirts swish about until, feeling giddy, she fell back onto the sofa.

'Oh dear, Papa,' she gasped, slightly breathless. 'I can feel your frown, even now. That raised eyebrow of yours, your twitching moustache, all those nice touches that made me feel so loved. Hah.' She broke into a fit of the giggles. 'That was a joke, Papa. You didn't know I could be so funny, did you? Of course, you didn't. I was your biggest disappointment; isn't that right, Papa? The ugly duckling that nobody

The Return

wanted, wasn't I? *Wasn't I, Papa?'*

Margot looked at Bessie and frowned. 'That poor woman. It doesn't sound like she's had a lot of affection in her life, if she had any at all.'

'Daughters married who their father chose, whether they liked it or not,' Bessie told her. 'It were Richard's title her father wanted, and Richard wanted his money. So, it were a match made in Heaven, so to speak. Mr Turnbull, he'd made his fortune trading, but that were frowned upon in the snobby-upper-classes. He weren't good enough for the likes of the lords and such. Titles open doors. With his daughter's marriage, he hoped to be more accepted.'

Bessie was about to say more but stopped when something Gwendolyn said caught her attention.

'You didn't think your plain daughter had a brain, did you, Papa? How fortuitous it was to discover we had hemlock growing in the garden. You thought it was a ridiculous pastime for a woman to be studying plants, didn't you? Needlework and reading poetry, that's all you said women were fit for. You really should have paid more attention, Papa.'

Gwendolyn heaved herself off the sofa and went to replenish her empty glass. With her face revealing all the hate she'd felt for him, she stared once more at her father's portrait, before turning and walking out of the room with her newly filled glass.

It was silent for a moment, neither saying a word.

Not until a thought struck Margot.

'Hemlock. Isn't that plant highly poisonous? Do you think she murdered her father?' Both women stared at the door, as if expecting Gwendolyn to come back with the answer, then turned, as one, and looked up at the portrait of Gwendolyn's father.

'I's not knowing and I's don't want to. Come on, let's get outta this place. I's not liking it here anymore.'

'Agreed. I don't know about you, but I'm feeling really tired. Is there somewhere we can go to rest up for a while?'

'I's thinking we's be going to Lord Brandon's house now. You can rest a bit while I's be snooping around.'

'Don't you want to sleep? It's been a long day; you must be just as tired as I am.'

Bessie gave Margot that mysterious smile that matched the twinkle in her eyes.

'I's never tired, dearie, so's don't you go fretting about me. Come on, let's go.'

Margot just stared, then rolled her eyes. She knew the subject was closed and that was that.

*****

Miles woke before Meg and gently eased himself out of the bed. He opened and closed the door with just as much care, then slipped out to make his way to the second bedroom where he'd left his clothes and other

The Return

personal items.

Half an hour later, he strode into the kitchen, startling the girl who was firing up the range before the cook arrived. A kettle, hanging from the cooking crane over the open fire in the corner of the room, was already boiling away.

'Good morning, Jane. Don't worry about me, just carry on as if I wasn't here.' Miles went across to the fire and, grabbing a cloth, he removed the brass kettle from the crane and made himself a pot of tea, much to the surprise and consternation of the young girl.

Miles caught her watching, and smiled at the look of horror on her face. 'Did you think I didn't know how to make a pot of tea, Jane? Let me tell you, young lady, it was something I learned when I was just a mere lad. I'd watch our cook make it in the afternoon for my mother.'

Jane didn't say anything; she was too nervous. It wasn't normal for a Lord to come into the kitchen.

Miles realised he was frightening the girl, and carrying his cup, he walked towards the door. 'I'll leave you to get on, then.' And with a cheery smile, he left her standing, jaw hanging, by the cooking range.

He stood in the garden and drank his tea before going up to see if Meg was awake. He had a busy day ahead, and needed to leave now, but not before letting Meg know. When he went into her room, he found her up and sitting at her dresser, brushing her hair out.

'Good morning, my love,' he said. Walking up to her, he bent over and moved her hair aside so he could kiss her neck. He felt her breath catch, and smiled. 'I have to leave you for a while, but I'll return later this afternoon. Will you be all right?'

He moved around and leant against her dresser so he could see her face. *Will I ever be bored looking into your eyes, my dear one? No, never.*

Meg stood up and leaned against him. 'Of course, I'll be all right. What have you planned for the day? Or is it private work business?'

'No, nothing that interesting, but necessity dictates I sign some boring forms my solicitor has sent me, and they are all at my father's.' He smiled into her upturned face and kissed the tip of her nose. 'Have I ever told you how adorable your nose is?'

Meg laughed, easing away from his arms. 'Go on with you. I'll wait for your return and perhaps we can walk around the garden?'

'That sounds perfect.' He pulled her back and kissed her with a passion that even surprised him.

*****

When Margot woke up the following morning, she couldn't remember where she was for a moment. Ihad been dark when she and Bessie had arrived at Lord Brandon's mansion, so she hadn't been able to see anything.

The Return

Now, as she slowly came to, she recalled Bessie leading her into the bedroom and telling her to get some sleep. The room was lovely. The four-poster bed she'd slept on was harder than she was used to, but still comfortable.

She climbed out of bed, climbing being the operative word. She'd never slept in such a high bed. Margot still had all her clothes on, not sure if someone would find her there and want answers. She still wasn't used to this invisible business. Not being a ghost and still being solid, she had to be careful what she touched or moved. All of which made the invisible part implausible. Yet she knew it was true.

Margot was about to go searching for Bessie, when there was a tap on the door and her friend walked into the room.

'Good morning, how did you sleep?'

'Fine. This is a lovely bedroom, isn't it? I feel like royalty sleeping in here.' Margot said brightly. 'What did you get up to while I was sleeping?'

'I's been looking in Lord Brandon's office and I's found something very interesting. But before I tell you, let's go downstairs and have a little wander around.'

From what Margot had seen of this bedroom, she was looking forward to seeing the rest of the mansion. She had thought Richard's home was grand, but this one made it pale into insignificance. Where Richard's house screamed money; Lord Brandon's showed elegance and good taste.

'Wow!' There was nothing else Margot could say. The rooms were spacious, with ceiling to floor curtains, and beautiful furniture in the reception room, as well as the sitting room. The library must have had at least a thousand books on its shelves.

The dining room had to be the most majestic room of the mansion. The huge table had three beautiful silver candelabras set at appropriate distances apart and, with eighteen elegant dining chairs around it, it would be possible to accommodate their guests comfortably.

The walls were covered with incredible paintings, and several gilded mirrors to reflect the candlelight. Quality silverware, porcelain and glass were much in evidence, ready for the waiting staff to prepare the table. *The word "stunning" doesn't do it justice.*

Bessie chuckled, and patted Margot's arm. 'Now, this is what I's be calling classy. Lady Brandon watched over everything, right down to the oil lamps and the smallest candle.'

Margot was very impressed with the design of the home, but had other things on her mind. 'Okay, so are you going to tell me what you found that was so interesting?'

When Bessie's bright, sparkling eyes lit up, Margot knew she'd found something a tad more than interesting. 'Come on then, don't keep it to yourself.'

The Return

'Let's just say for now, Meg's father didn't lose his money gambling.'

13

'What?' Margot stopped dead. 'I don't think I heard you right. Did you say you found something that proves Meg's father *didn't* lose his money gambling?'

'Yes, you's hearing it right. It's all down on paper. I's thinking Miles' dad has been telling a few black lies.'

Margot frowned as she took a moment to digest this new piece of information. Then the frown deepened. 'But wasn't it the family solicitor who told them about Lord Crawford's gambling? Are you saying he lied, too?'

Bessie nodded. 'That's exactly what I's saying. And that got me thinking, why would a solicitor be doing that? We have to pay that man a visit.

The Return

Something is mighty wrong here.'

'You're telling *me* there's something wrong. What was it that led you to this conclusion, anyway?'

'Some papers I's finding while poking around in the library. They were in a locked cupboard. Of course, that got me wondering why would anyone want to lock a cupboard? It wouldn't be for a mop and bucket, now, would it? I's thinking there must be something of interest inside. It weren't hard to open.'

'You broke the lock? Won't someone see it's been opened?'

Bessie pointed to the pins in her hair, and grinned. 'A tweak and a twiddle and it were soon open. And were it worth it? My word, it was. It was stacked high with files; some looked to be there for years. It's all above my head, but this is roughly how I's understanding it. Lord Crawford and Lord Brandon put money into something and then later Lord Brandon took his money all out again without telling Lord Crawford. Lord Brandon lost nothing, and Lord Crawford lost his whole estate.'

'Why would he do that ... unless he knew something that Lord Crawford didn't, and forgot to pass it on.' Margot stood up and walked around the bedroom. 'I want to read that document. Where is it?'

'Still down in the library room. There's lots more papers, but I's not understanding all the mumbo jumbo jargon. It's another language to me.'

Margot smiled. 'I know what you mean. I need a dictionary beside me when it comes to official documents. Getting back to this solicitor, what I still don't understand is why would he tell Lady Crawford and her children such an outright lie? If it came out, he could lose his qualifying law degree, and that would effectively ruin him.'

'That's right. There's more to this than we's knowing. And you's going to find out what it is.'

'Me? Now just you hang on a minute. How in heaven's name am I going to do that?'

Bessie shrugged and turned away. 'I's still thinking on it.'

'Well, while you're thinking, you can show me where the document is.' Margot was already moving towards the door.

First impressions are usually lasting, and Margot's impression of the library had taken her by surprise. She'd been mesmerised by the grandeur and size of the room. The full shelves, spanning from floor to ceiling, needed the moving step ladders to get to those books that were out of reach.

Now that Bessie's overnight search had discovered more items of interest hidden away in a cupboard, Margot couldn't wait to go back and see them for herself.

'I's thinking we's have to be careful; we's don't want anyone to see cupboards being opened and papers being removed by themselves. It were easy for me with everyone in their beds,' Bessie reminded Margot as they went down the stairs.

Even though it would be hilarious, Margot agreed to be careful when people were around. The library was empty when they went into the room, and Bessie went straight over to the cupboard. Taking one of her hairpins, she once again picked the lock.

'Here we are,' she said, turning around with the papers she'd read and waving them in front of Margot's face. 'These has all the proof we's needing to show that Lord Crawford didn't gamble his fortune away.'

Margot took the documents and sat down at the reading table. They were official documents, signed by both the solicitor and Lord Brandon, and although she didn't understand much of the legal terminology, she could see that Lord Brandon had stitched Lord Crawford up good and proper.

'What a bastard.' Margot was furious. 'Why would he do such a thing to his son's future father-in-law?'

'Perhaps he didn't want Miles to marry Meg. I's don't know. What I's *do* know is, he's not going to get away with it. We's getting all this out in the open. Richard'll be furious.'

Margot could just imagine how Richard would react to this revelation. 'Yes, I agree with you. But we also have to find out who wants Meg dead.'

'Hmm. I's thinking that once we get to the bottom of this little mystery, we'll likely get an answer to that one, as well.'

'You could be right. So have you had enough time to come up with a way to do it?'

'Yes … But I's thinking that, without realising or understanding, you's already knew what had to be done from that moment you's stepped into your new home.'

That threw Margot. 'I don't understand. What and how could I possibly have known?'

'It's simple really. You and Meg have one of thems invisible link thingies that's joined you together. A bit like us, I s'pose. We's here, but no one can see us. You can feel what Meg feels, and that's why you had all them longings for Miles' spirit. He's knowing you'd not be able to resist him, and that was why you agreed to come here.'

There was a long silence as Margot thought this one through. *Bessie's right, I do feel a connection with Meg.* 'Okay, supposing I agree with what you're saying, how does that help us with this problem?'

Bessie studied Margot for a moment. Her usual twinkling eyes dulled as she tried to think of a way to say what she had to. She took a deep breath and forced a smile.

'What I's not told you before is … well … Look, there isn't any easy way to say this, so I's just going

The Return

to say it. The closer you get to Meg, the more you'll become her until you's finally merged and become one person. … are you still with me?'

Margot's eyes were the size of saucers. She stared at Bessie wondering where she'd escaped from. 'This is crazy. I'm sorry, Bessie, but no, you've completely lost me.'

Bessie sat down at the table with Margot. 'I's thinking as much. Let me try to make it clearer. … Please listen to what I's got to say. It's important.'

Margot looked into Bessie's clear, warm eyes, and knew the many questions that she'd asked before, and which Bessie had dismissed, were now going to be answered. She nodded and sat upright, preparing herself. 'Okay, I'll listen.'

'Good.' Bessie reached over and patted Margot's hand. 'Because this'll sound even more crazy. You's might have been hearing of this before and not believed it, but there *are* more timelines running side by side. Your timeline's all good. But cause Meg were murdered in her timeline and shouldn't have, everything got changed. That's why we's here today; we's got to make it right.'

Bessie couldn't help but smile at the befuddled look on Margot's face. 'Now we's over that part, I's be telling you the rest. Meg and Miles should've married. Meg will save the life of a young lad whose descendant plays an important role in medicine.

Whoever's planning to murder Meg has gotta be stopped. The future depends on it.'

When Bessie had finished talking, she sat back and stared at Margot, waiting for her reaction. 'Whatever you's choosing to believe, what I's just told you is the gospel truth.'

Margot stood up and paced the room, trying to get her head around all this. She knew the moment she saw the house, way in the future, that she belonged there. She knew Miles, even though she didn't. And then there was Meg. Yes, she did feel that connection. Margot looked at Bessie and made her decision.

'Okay, I'll do it. But I've got a few questions, and if you can answer them, you'll have my full cooperation. What happens to me when this is all over? Will I become me again? Will I be able to go back to my own timeline?'

Bessie smiled and walked over and stood in front of Margot, taking both her hands in hers. 'I's promising you now, Margot, you *will* go back to your own timeline. We's just got to sort this lot out and get everyone's life back on track.'

'Okay then, let's do this.' Now the decision was made, Margot was excited. *At least I get to be with Miles for a while.*

Voices from the other side of the door had them both look up. 'That's Miles,' Bessie said, quickly returning the document to the file, closing the door and locking it.

The Return

*****

Miles went straight to his room, washed and put on a clean set of clothes. His mind was full of his surprise Christmas wedding and couldn't wait to get started. He'd need to talk to his friend, Joshua Fellows. Miles wanted him to be his best man and knew he could trust him to keep the secret.

First, he had another job to do, and that couldn't wait. After Meg's shattering
statement that she had no friends anymore, he'd decided to rectify that as well. To do this, he needed to speak to Lucy Shivers, Meg's once best friend. He was going to give Meg a birthday to remember. He had lots to do, and not much time to do it. Suddenly life looked good.

*****

Meg was having her breakfast when Margot and Bessie arrived at the house. It seemed weird to Margot seeing all the ornaments, pictures and ornate mirrors on the wall that were still in the house when she moved in over a hundred years later.

Bessie nudged Margot, bringing her out of her daydreaming. 'I's thinking you'd do good if you study Meg today. Watch the way she does things, eats, walks, talks, especially what she's like with them that works for her. This is important if we's going to pull this off.'

'Good idea.' Margot stared at Meg for a while,

amazed at the likeness they shared. She was also aware of the sadness in Meg's eyes, and a feeling of acute compassion assailed her.

Even if it means I have to give up my life in the future, I will do everything in my power to make her happy again.

The Return

14

Margot kept her distance from Meg but stayed close enough to watch how she carried herself, and to hear her speak, which was mostly to the staff. It wasn't long before Margot was shown how much respect and affection they had for their mistress. But it was the sadness in Meg's eyes that caught her attention.

'I do hope this works,' Margot said softly.

'It will,' Bessie replied. ''I's thinking that tomorrow, we'll go and see that so-called solicitor. You keep watching Meg, cause you's going to merge with her tonight when she's asleep.'

'Do you think I'll be ready by then? It's not as if she's said much since we've been here.' Now the time to do this was fast approaching, Margot found she was more than a little nervous about the task ahead of her.

'Oh, and another question, will I be able to see you when I'm Meg?'

Bessie smiled and nodded. 'Yes. I's thinking it wouldn't be a good idea to be letting you loose on your own.'

Bessie heard Margot's big sigh and realised how nervous she was getting. She smiled and went over to give her a comforting hug. 'You's going to be fine, so stop all this fretting.'

The day continued slowly without anything noticeable happening that Margot needed to worry about. Soon it was time for Meg to retire, and the knots in Margot's stomach started to play havoc with her nerves.

If I get through this, it will be a miracle.

It didn't take long before Meg's gentle, rhythmic breathing told Margot and Bessie that she was sound asleep.

'So, what happens now?' Margot asked brightly, trying her hardest not to
sound concerned, as if it was a natural everyday occurrence to hop in and out of
someone else's body.

'Just move towards the bed, slowly, don't rush it.'

As if I would. Margot moved forward, each step dragging as slow as was physically possible without going backwards. She turned and looked at Bessie, who gave her an encouraging nod. *Okay, I can do this.*

The Return

Margot stood straight, threw her shoulders back and, closing her eyes, she stepped forward.

As she moved closer, a weird feeling hit her as thousands of pins and needles prickled every part of her body. For a wild terrifying moment, Margot thought her body was disintegrating. She wanted to cry out ... call Bessie ... tell her she'd changed her mind ... but couldn't open her mouth.

Just as Margot thought she was going to die, all the horrendous sensations ceased and, at the same moment, her physical awareness faded before a final rush grabbed hold and sucked her in ... and then nothing.

Oh, what happened? Why is it so dark? Bessie didn't tell me it would be dark. ... Am I still me or have I turned into Meg? I feel so tired ... Where's Bessie? I'm ... so ... sleepy ... Why am I so tired? ... Am I me? ... Where is Meg, is she here, too? ... Does she know I'm here?... Where am I? ... Am I me?

****

The suddenness of glaring light woke Margot with a start. It took a moment to remember where she was and what she'd done. She raised herself up onto her elbows and saw Bessie pulling back the curtains.

'Rise and shine, Mistress Meg.' Bessie came over to the bed and looked down at Margot. 'How're you feeling?'

Sandra Stoner-Mitchell

Margot pulled herself up into a sitting position and stared at her friend. 'It's me, not Meg, and I'm feeling fine … I think.' Margot said, more than just a little irritated.

'I know it's you. But you've got to get used to people calling you Meg or this whole thing'll end before we's started.' Bessie went over to where the washbowl was and felt the water. 'If'n you're quick, you'll get your wash in before the girl comes to help you.'

'Great.' Margot swung her legs out onto the freezing floor, then immediately pulled them back again. 'Damn. That's cold. Does Meg have a pair of slippers, or some socks?'

'Yes, they's here, but don't be looking that comfortable.' Bessie bent down
and picked up a pair of slippers not unlike ballet shoes in shape, but very hard. 'Here's you are.'

Margot brought her legs up under her chin and put them on. 'What's happened to Meg now that I'm in her body? Does she know I've invaded her space?'

'No, Meg's self is sleeping. She won't wake up till you's leaving her. But she's going to know everything you's done because her brain will keep the memory. Meg'll remember it as if she did it all.'

'I did wonder about that. I'd hate to think she'd come round believing she'd gone crazy.'

'Come on, we's got a lot to do. A girl will be

coming soon to help you into your dress.'

By the time Margot had dressed, breakfasted, and had her carriage brought to the door, nearly two hours had passed. She couldn't help but compare it to her usual rush in the mornings getting ready for work.

Now, sitting in her carriage, being taken to see her family solicitor, she was able to ask Bessie if she could remember the solicitor's name that had been on the document she'd found. It had been worrying her all through breakfast.

'Mr Crankston-Smythe. Do you know what you's going to say to him?'

Margot studied her gloved hands before giving an answer. 'I've been thinking about that, too. I think it would be best if I just get straight to the point. I've no interest in idle chit-chat. I'm there to get some answers, and he'd better be giving me some.'

'I's thinking that's best, too. We's nearly there. Are you ready?'

'Yes, and no. I wish you could be seen, too. I'd be a lot happier,' Margot said, anxiously. 'At least having you in the flesh, so to speak, you'd be giving me some confidence.'

Bessie was silent for a moment. 'I's thinking it'll be better this way. How would you explain me suddenly appearing?'

Margot nodded. She knew it would be too much to expect. She felt the coach slow, then jolt to a stop.

Sandra Stoner-Mitchell

Margot looked out of the window and watched as the driver knocked on the solicitor's door, before returning to help her down.

The door was opened by a rather stiff doorman. Margot wondered if his face would have split in two had he attempted to smile. She introduced herself, and he went off to let Mr Crankston-Smythe know she was there. Within moments the man in question came through, his face alight with a smile.

'My dear Lady Margaret, how nice of you to grace my home. Please, come on through. I shall send for refreshments immediately.' He nodded towards his doorman who turned and hurried away.

Margaret? Margot pretended to look around but gave Bessie a discreet quizzical look.

'Margaret is her proper name, Meg was Lord Crawford's pet name for her,' Bessie explained, knowing only Margot could hear. 'And now, of course, Miles calls her it as well.'

Mr Crankston-Smythe led her into his office. After seeing she was comfortably seated in the sumptuous leather chair in front of his desk, he turned on his heal and walked around to his own.

'Now, what can I do for you? It's been a long time; what is it now? Ten years?'

'Eight, actually.' Margot snapped back. 'That's what I wanted to talk to you about.'

'Oh? Perhaps you'll enlighten me. Let me get my

pen so I can take notes. Now, what is it that you want to discuss?'

'We'll start with my father's so-called gambling, shall we?' Margot said, hoping to see some sort of reaction, but was sorely disappointed.

'So-called gambling? Ah, I can understand how upsetting that must have been for you all.' He looked down at the pen in his hand and began doodling on his pad. 'I will remember the look of shock and disbelief on your mother's face for the rest of my days,' he said, his voice barely above a whisper. 'But there was nothing I could have said that would have helped her.'

'Really? Perhaps if you'd told us the truth it might have. You'd known my father for years; he was a friend as well as your client for heaven's sake. Yet you showed him no loyalty whatsoever when he needed it most.'

Watching Mr Crankston-Smythe's expression as he studied her face whilst keeping his own unreadable, Margot's temper was on the verge of exploding. She needed to remain calm.

When he spoke this time, his tone was firm and somewhat angry. 'I understand your faith in your father has been somewhat tested, but you must believe me when I tell you there was nothing I could have done to stop his gambling; don't you think I would have done so had I been able? Yes, he was my friend, but circumstances tied my hands.'

'My father didn't gamble; you know that as well as I do. He was too honourable a man. But he did go into a business partnership with Lord Brandon, didn't he? Please don't deny it.' *Ha. That's got you. Get out of that.*

He stood and walked around to where Margot was sitting. 'I think you should leave.'

'Not until I get the truth out of you. You deliberately ruined my father's good name; you and Lord Brandon are monsters.' Margot stood up and faced him, her anger boiling over. 'You let my family suffer all those years, and I want to know why.'

'I have nothing more to say. If you have any more questions, you should put them to Lord Brandon yourself. Now, if you will excuse me, I have a busy day ahead.'

He was about to go to the door when a movement stopped him. As he looked over Margot's head, his face paled, his eyes terror-stricken....

The Return

15

When Margot turned her head to see what had frightened Mr Crankston-Smythe so badly, it was all she could do to stop herself from laughing. Instead, she put her hand over her mouth and coughed to suppress the chuckle as she realised what it was he thought he was seeing.

'I's thinking it would be fun if'n he thinks I's the ghost of Meg's father. That'll be getting some answers,' Bessie explained as she waved a piece of paper above her head. Then, seeing the pen, she picked it up, twirled it in the air like a baton, caught it, and threw it at the hapless solicitor who yelped and ducked.

Margot couldn't control the laughter any longer. 'Papa.' she cried, going along with Bessie's little subterfuge. 'You followed me. That was naughty of you. Can't you see you're scaring the life out of Mr Cranky-Smythe?'

Bessie laughed at that. 'I's thinking that's what we's be calling him from now on. Mr Cranky has a ring to it.'

When Margot turned back towards him, her laughter came to an abrupt end. Her expressive eyes narrowed ominously. 'I'm afraid dear Papa is rather angry. He never did like liars.'

She watched his ashen face go blotchy as his terror increased. *Oh Meg, I do so hope you will find this 'memory' as exquisite as I do when you take over again.*

'I … Lord Crawford is here? That … that's his gho … ghost?'

Enjoying the effect she was having on him, Bessie decided to intensify her ghostly efforts and petrify him more. She wouldn't stop until he begged for mercy and agreed to tell them what he knew. First to be targeted were all the items on the desk. With one sweep of her hand, she sent everything flying, including the full inkwell which splattered the wall and carpet.

It was then she spotted the solicitor's portrait hanging in pride of place where everyone could see it. It was quite large. Bessie estimated the weight was within her capability to lift it off the wall. Once in her hands, she realised just how heavy it was, but that didn't deter her, especially when she saw the look of horror on Mr Crankston-Smythe's face.

Still keeping her cheerful grin, she managed to stagger across the room and stand in front of him. It was getting heavier by the second. When she almost dropped it, the solicitor, now worried about his precious portrait, instinctively made a grab for it, and, holding it tight, he tugged hard. Bessie was also determined to keep hold of it, refusing to let go, which made him even more hell-bent on taking it away from the invisible "Lord Crawford's ghost."

When Bessie *did* let go, he was caught by surprise and stumbled backwards, barely able to keep his balance and nearly dropping the portrait.

'Oh Papa, please try to control yourself. I think you have frightened Mr Crankston-Smythe enough. I'm sure he will be keen to talk to us now,' she turned to the solicitor, 'won't you?'

By now, the man was a total mess. His head jerked from where he thought the ghost was, over to the door. Margot watched his body rock, as if he was preparing to make a run for it.

'I think you should talk to me before my father loses his temper,' Margot said softly.

The hapless solicitor gazed at the door and then, to his utter dismay, he watched as a piece of paper floated past him, only to stop in front of his only escape route. The thought of walking through a ghost made him feel physically sick and the idea was dismissed without further consideration.

With his shoulders slumped in defeat, he moved back to sit on his chair, then, setting his elbows on the desk, he dropped his face into his hands.

Bessie sat on the desk with a satisfied grin, as Margot sat back in the chair. 'I's thinking that should about do it. The little weasel. Perhaps we'll get the truth out of him now.'

Mr Crankston-Smythe sat up and opened one of his desk drawers, pulled out a bottle of brandy and a glass, which he filled and immediately drank. Without even looking at Margot, he filled the glass again and then held the stem between his fingers so the balloon fit snugly in the palm of his hand. He stared at the golden liquid for a moment and then, as if he'd come to some sort of decision, he took a sip and put the glass back down on the desk.

Leaning back into his chair, he slowly raised his eyes and stared at Margot. 'I don't know what you hope to achieve by bringing all this up now, Lady Margaret. Apart from creating another scandal, which I'm sure you don't want, the outcome would still be the same. Regardless of how your father went bankrupt, it would still have happened, and he would still have shot himself. 'He looked around the room, himself.' He looked around the as if looking for Meg's father's ghost. 'I think you should try to discourage your daughter's foolhardiness, Lord Crawford,' he said, talking to thin air. 'Unless, of course, you don't care about her ruining her own name as well?'

He turned to Margot and grinned. 'Whatever proof of my wrongdoing you might think you have, I can guarantee, here and now, you will come off worse; I will make sure of it. Your father's name will be dragged through the mud again, and you will most certainly be ostracised for your part in this whole sordid affair. So, do your worst. Let's see who will believe the daughter of a known bankrupt.'

Margot felt her temper rising, and tried hard to keep it under control. She had to behave like Lady Margaret, and right at this moment, she was finding that very hard to do.

Bessie could see the rage in Margot's eyes, and quickly stepped in. 'I's thinking we'll go and see what other proof we can find, and then we's can act on it.' She looked at the solicitor as he sat at his desk smirking. 'Give me a hand with this bloody portrait,' she said, moving over to where it was leaning against his chair.

Margot stared at her and then the picture. She didn't say anything, but followed Bessie around the desk, and had the satisfaction of seeing fear reappear in the grubby solicitor's eyes.

'Get one side of it and then help me lift it above

his head.'

Margot smiled, realising what Bessie had in mind. Before Mr Cranky had time to move, they lifted the picture and brought it down over his head. Then turned and quickly left the room to the sounds of him howling obscene and slanderous names.

'I's thinking that's got him stirred up a bit.' Bessie laughed.

'Do you know what, I don't like the idea of him thinking he has one over us.' Margot stopped and looked back at the solicitor's door. 'And I don't like the way he's speaking. I'm going back.'

'What? Wait a minute, what are you going to do?'

'Watch and learn.' Margot stomped off and entered the solicitor's room and, seeing Bessie had followed close behind, she slammed the door and marched up to his desk.

The solicitor immediately stopped his ranting. He'd removed the ruined picture, and now stood up ready to do battle with the woman glaring up at him.

'Mr Crankston-Smythe, where I come from, corruption is frowned upon and dealt with harshly, and you, sir, are the most corrupt person I've had the misfortune to meet. I am not Lady Margaret, but I am here looking after her interests, and let me tell you, I'll make damned sure you end your career in prison. I know all about you and your business venture with Lord Brandon, *and* how between you, you both

The Return

deliberately stitched up Lord Crawford so he would lose his entire fortune. I know a lot more than you realise, you piece of scum. And, furthermore, I shall make sure you, and that conniving sonofabitch friend of yours, lives to regret it. Do you understand me?'

Margot glared dangerously at the man, now sitting with his mouth dropped open. 'You, sir, are a disgrace to your profession.' With that, Margot turned on her heel and marched across the room to where Bessie stood with the door already opened. 'Let's get out of here before I do something I might regret.'

The carriage was waiting when they left the solicitor's office and soon they were on their way home. It was only then that Margot let herself relax. She grinned, then chuckled, and finally, she laughed so hard it made her sides hurt.

Bessie stared and shook her head, but her lips did start to curl. 'What was you thinking? Just wait until he tells Lord Brandon.'

Margot stopped laughing, but the huge grin remained. 'And what will he say? Will he tell him that a woman, who just happened to look exactly like Lady Margaret, came to visit him today with Lord Crawford's ghost, and then repeat what I said? Can you imagine how that would make him look?'

Bessie thought about it, and the smile broadened. 'I's thinking you's right. Oh, how I'd like to hear that conversation.'

'Yes, I would, too. But now we have to get the proof we need to show Miles. Until then, we can't do anything. That document would help, but it's not enough to prove Lord Brandon did anything wrong.' Margot frowned. 'All we have is the document to say what he did, but if we give that to Miles, his father could easily argue that he'd told Lord Crawford, and he hadn't listened.'

They both sat silent, swaying to the motion of the wheels turning, and the occasional jolt when they hit a rut in the road.

'He'd have to explain why Lord Crawford had written a suicide note saying he'd gambled the money away, too. Obviously, that hadn't been the case. And, now I come to think of it, did Lord Crawford actually write that note? I mean, it was Mr Crankston-Smythe who read it out at the reading of the will.'

The Return

16

As the carriage pulled up outside Margot's home, she noticed Miles' horse tethered to the post outside the stables, happily munching on what was left of the grass. The summer heat had destroyed most of it, but the recent winter downpours had managed to restore what had survived.

'Miles is here. What should I say to him?' Margot was both excited and nervous. This would be the real test; would she be convincing enough to carry off her portrayal of Meg?

'I's thinking he won't be staying long, or he'd have stabled his horse and not left it outside.' Bessie patted Margot's knee. 'Just act normal and you'll be fine.'

When the carriage door opened, Margot's stomach

somersaulted. 'Miles. I'm sorry, was I expecting you?' Then, blushing to the roots of her red hair, she realised how rude that sounded. 'Not that it isn't lovely to see you,' she added, lowering her head to hide her embarrassment.

Miles roared with laughter at her confusion. 'No, my dear, I hadn't made any arrangements to visit with you today. It was a spur of the moment decision. Come here, my little treasure; how I've missed you.'

With that he wrapped his large hands around her waist and lifted her out of the carriage.

'Have you been anywhere special, or just escaping for a while?' he asked, still holding her so her feet weren't touching the ground.

Margot was quick to put her thoughts in place, not wanting to mention her visit to the solicitor just yet. With a coy tilt of her head, she looked up at him and fluttered her eyelids in a playful manner.

'That's only for me to know, sir. A lady must keep some mystery about herself or else her gentleman friend will soon become bored. Now are you going to put me down? Or must I call for the cavalry?'

'Now that would be boring,' he told her, still laughing. 'Come on, let's get inside. I have something to ask you.'

'Oh? And that sounds mysterious,' she said, joining in with his laughter.

When they'd been relieved of their coats, they

The Return

walked into the sitting room where Margot was pleased to see the fire roaring up the chimney. She went over and held out her hands towards the warmth.

'That feels better.' Once her hands had thawed, she turned and faced Miles. 'Now you must tell me what you want to ask of me. It must be important for you to come all this way.'

It took Miles two strides to be standing in front of her. 'It's always important when it comes to being with you, my sweet Meg.' Putting one arm around her waist, he pulled her close. His other hand stroked the side of her face. 'Do you have any idea of just how much I love you?'

His words made her tremble. For a moment, she allowed herself to forget it was Meg he believed he was talking to, and not her. Then his lips came down and captured hers. There was no way on earth she could pull away, nor did she want to.

If this is what it's like to be in Heaven, please let me stay forever.

It was then that she remembered Bessie was in the room and watching their every move. What had been a lovely interlude, she now brought to an end. Margot gently disengaged herself from his arms, still staring up into his eyes.

I still can't get over how tall you are ... and you're much too handsome to be allowed out on your own.

She sighed with real regret. He wasn't hers to drool over.

'If that's what your question is, then it wouldn't matter how many times you asked me, I would still enjoy hearing it,' she murmured while trying to put on a bright smile.

Then she saw Bessie giving a thumbs up signal and grinning her head off. 'I's thinking you's got him fooled.'

But that's not what I want to do. I want him to be mine. Why, oh why, did I agree to do this?

Miles was smiling at her. 'Although I meant every word, that wasn't what I wanted to ask. Come, sit by my side.' He held onto her hand and led her over to the sofa.

'This sounds very serious, Miles. Is everything all right?'

He smiled and dropped a kiss on the tip of her nose. 'Yes, everything is perfect. I want to tell you a little story about my grandparents as it's relevant to what I truly want to ask.'

'Then I shall sit here quietly and listen.' Margot smiled and sat back, making herself comfortable.

'Back in their day it was most unusual for a couple to marry for love. It was more to do with boosting the fortunes, or opportunities, of both families. As it was, my grandparents loved each other dearly.'

Margot noticed how his smile lit up his whole face

The Return

as he spoke of them. She couldn't help but smile as well.

'After my grandmother had accepted my grandfather's proposal of marriage, he gave her a ring that was worn on her right hand until their wedding day. It was then taken off and put on the ring finger of her left hand.'

'How romantic. I've never heard of that before. Would that be her wedding ring or engagement ring?'

'Both, I suppose. She also had two simple gold *keeper* rings, which are worn on both sides of the main ring to enhance and protect it. I can still see the pride in her face when she talked about it. They had a long and very loving marriage, one that I dearly want to emulate. When my grandmother died, part of my inheritance was her rings. She wanted me to give them to the lady who would be my forever love.'

Miles put his hand in his pocket and brought out a small velvet bag. He untied the silk cord and emptied the contents onto his hand. 'You are that lady, my sweet Meg. I have never stopped loving you, and I never will. Will you wear this ring on your right hand until we are married?'

Margot's eyes dropped from his to the ring he now held between his fingers. It was gold, with a delicate filigree pattern, inset with a little posy of coloured gemstones, rubies, sapphires, amethyst, and garnet. It was stunning. Her eyes flickered across to Bessie.

'I's thinking you must say what Mistress Meg would say, and we's both knows what that would be.'

Margot looked up and smiled. 'Oh, Miles, I am humbled that you've chosen me to wear your grandmother's ring. It symbolises everything I've dreamed my married life would be based on. Her ring is so lovely. I will wear it with love and honour. I only wish I could have met your grandparents—' Margot's face suddenly clouded over.

'What is it, my love?' Miles watched the conflicting thoughts passing over her face.

'I'm wondering if they would have approved of you giving me these rings? Knowing what your parents think of me, wouldn't they feel the same? Perhaps I shouldn't accept this; we'll never get married, will we?'

It was now Miles' face that changed. His eyes flashed dangerously. 'I've had just about enough of my parents' interference in my affairs. I know my grandparents would have loved you, and would have welcomed you into the family with arms open wide. We will get married, my sweet Meg, and no one will stop us.'

He took her right hand and slipped the first keeper ring on her finger followed by the beautiful wedding-engagement ring, and finally, the second keeper ring. 'See. They were made for you,' he told her, and she had to agree. They fitted her finger perfectly.

The Return

'It's beautiful, Miles,' she whispered, lightly touching the gemstones. Her eyes glistened as sadness overwhelmed her. Knowing that soon she would have to leave him, and the real owner of his love would take over once more, hurt her more than she could ever have imagined.

Miles stood up and pulled her up with him. 'Look, I can't stay. There are some people I have to meet. But I'll be back tonight.' He drew her into his arms and groaned. 'I hate leaving you, even for a few hours. But all that will change soon, my love.' He kissed her gently, sending little tremors flitting through her body.

When he'd left her, she collapsed on the sofa. Her emotions were like a tidal wave that threatened to overwhelm her. 'He's coming back tonight. What am I going to do?' She looked down at the rings on her finger. 'They're so beautiful, aren't they?' She held her arm out so Bessie could admire it.

'Yes, they certainly are,' Bessie agreed. 'Meg needs you to be strong, now, Margot. She deserves to be happy, not dead. I's going back to Lord Brandon's home tonight, and then on to that nasty Mr Cranky's. I'll be searching both their offices for anything that will get Cranky put away and show Lord Brandon up for what he is.'

She looked into Margot's face, and sighed. 'I's thinking you's fallen in love with our dashing Miles, and I's can't say as I's blames you. You's going to need all your strength to get through this. But you will, my dear, you will.'

The rest of the day passed far too quickly. Margot's mind was dreading Miles' return, while at the same time her body was remembering how he'd made her feel on those ghostly visits of his, back in her own time, and was already eagerly anticipating what was to come.

But this is different. I've never slept with a living man before. Only a ghost, I don't know what to do. He's going to know for sure that I'm not Meg. I am not ready for this.

The Return

17

Bessie went off to do her investigating later in the evening, leaving Margot alone with her thoughts. Which was not helping at all. The more she thought about Miles coming back for the night, the more nervous she was getting.

After a while, she decided she would go to her room and get changed into her nightgown. She called for Jane, her young lady's maid, to help her out of her dress. They were such complicated affairs.

The many frills and bows, buttons, and goodness knows what else to undo, was just the beginning. The huge bustle at the back with its wire cage and straps to hold it in place, was the hardest part to get out of on her own. And she hated it with a passion.

I will never wonder if my bottom looks too big again. How women used to think this bustle style was attractive, I don't know, and it's darned uncomfortable as well.

Jane was a shy young girl, who barely spoke two words while she was helping her mistress out of her clothes. Margot was glad of the silence; she was too nervous for small talk.

I am just glad Miles isn't here yet, at least I won't have to take all this off in front of him. Perhaps, with any luck, I'll have fallen asleep before he comes ... Now, that's just you being a coward. Margot admonished herself. She threw her head back and groaned, causing Jane to jump.

'Sorry, Mistress.'

Margot looked at her frightened face and smiled. 'It's all right , Jane, it was nothing you did,' she assured her. 'Go on, I can manage the rest now you've got the dress and corset off. I'll see you in the morning.'

After Jane had left the room, Margot finished putting her nightdress on. *At least this is quite pretty and I can breathe in it.* She pushed the long cotton sleeves up to her elbow, fluffing out the lacy cuffs, then, seeing a brush on the dressing table, she went over and used it to tidy her hair.

'Okay, Margot, what now?' She looked over at the window where two easy chairs and a small oval table beckoned her. Too nervous to feel tired, Margot went

The Return

across and, pulling back the curtains, she sat and admired the clear, starlit sky.

When her gaze wandered, she noticed a book on the table and picked it up. It was poetry written by Elizabeth Barrett Browning. Margot opened it and turned the pages; they were poems of either love or terrible grief. One poem in particular caught her eye because she knew the words by heart.

'How do I love thee … How, indeed.' *I can't read these, not the way I'm feeling.* She closed the book and put it back on the table then looked across at the bed. *He wouldn't expect me to wait up all night, would he? No, he wouldn't.*

Margot made her decision and went across and climbed into bed. *What do people do in the evenings without the television? It can't be all balls and dinner parties.* She lay there for a while, her mind refusing to shut down.

I wish I had my watch; don't they have clocks in this era? Oh, for heaven's sake, Margot, get a grip. It's obvious he's not coming now. The thought caught her short. 'Well, how bloody rude.'

Then seeing the funny side of her righteous indignation, Margot started to laugh. 'You'll make your mind up one of these days. Do you want him to come, or not?' She didn't bother answering herself. Instead, satisfied she would be spending the night alone, she reached over and put the oil lamp out.

Sandra Stoner-Mitchell

Pulling the blankets up, she turned onto her side, and within minutes she was sound asleep.

*****

She knew he was here, felt his gentle hand push the hair from her face and then his lips came down and brushed her cheek. She moaned as his hand circled her waist, encouraging her to turn onto her back as his hand moved to stroke her breast.

He was teasing her again, as he always did ... she couldn't stand it ... but she didn't want him to stop. 'Miles,' her voice, so quiet, it was less than a whisper as she arched her back, inviting him to do what he wanted with her, to show her what she'd never experienced, she wanted it all ... she wanted to cry out, tell him
not to leave.

'My dearest, sweetest Meg,' he moaned, his voice was husky, urgent, but not demanding.

Margot's hands were moving over his bare shoulders, stroking his chest ... *I'm stroking his naked chest.* This had never happened before. This was no dream, it was *real ... Miles* was real. Her heart raced as she realised this time, he wouldn't leave her.

Her first impulse was to push him away, she wasn't Meg, surely this was wrong. Then she grabbed hold. All the rights and wrongs of the situation were dismissed, not caring, she loved him, it was right.

The Return

Her excitement built as she let her hands move over his body, her body trembled the further her hands moved over his glorious naked, muscular chest, down to his stomach … she heard his sharp intake of breath. Intoxicated with this unknown power she had over him she started to move lower still, but before she could, he grabbed her hand.

'Not so fast you little minx; now it's my time.' He pulled her up then whipped her nightdress off and threw it on the floor. 'That's better.' With one large hand, he imprisoned both hers and held them over her head, then kissed her, forcing her lips apart wider to allow his tongue to prod and explore her mouth.

Margot, never having been kissed this way before, felt her excitement soar. Her heartrate increased dramatically. Her whole body was alive and wanting.

She needed her hands to be free so she could touch him, too, and she tugged them out of Miles' control, but then he dropped his lips to her breasts and using his tongue again, he teased her nipples while his fingers played with her navel, sending exquisite sensations through her body.

With little feather-like touches, his fingers went further. Her hips lurched as feelings between her legs sent her quivering. She knew she was wet. She cried out, called his name and then her hand found him, his hardness shocked and excited her. Her mind was scrambled as he moved over her, and then, urgently, they were joined.

It was over so fast, Margot was left shuddering, disappointed, unsure of what had just happened, as Miles collapsed, gasping, on top of her.

A few seconds passed before Miles rolled off her and stroked the side of her face. 'I'm sorry, love, that was not supposed to have happened like that, but when you touched me, I completely lost control. That has never happened to me before.' He searched her face, looking for, what?

For one awful moment, Margot thought his memory was returning to his time
in the future with her. But his next words filled her with relief.

'You have me bewitched, my darling, Meg. Now it's my turn.' he murmured; the glint in his eye implied so much more.

Margot's eyes widened with anticipation, as he wrapped his arms around her and kissed her with such passion that she was left breathless.

'You are the most precious person in my life. I love you so much, my sweet Meg.'

Tiny shivers rippled through her body as she clung to him, never wanting to let him go. Her most intimate area still throbbed with wanton desire and desperate longing, more than she'd felt when he'd visited her as a ghost in her time.

His feathery kisses continued on her neck when

her head tipped back as he lowered her onto the pillow again.

Her heart, pounding like a crazed drummer, carried away with the moment, as every previously dormant perception her body possessed was brought to life. His touch alone made her want to cry tears of ecstasy. He was exploring her body, touching, kissing every part as if for the first time. She tried to touch him, but he stopped her.

Margot thought she'd felt all the sensuous, carnal feelings possible for a body to experience, until he brought her to the ultimate pleasure. Tears poured free as her body felt the explosive release of her first climax. It was beyond anything she could have imagined.

*****

Miles woke before Margot, who'd slept the whole night wrapped in his arms. He thought about their incredible love making; it was the best he'd ever enjoyed. That it was with the woman he loved beyond life itself, was not surprising.

He smiled, knowing they would be married soon, and he couldn't wait. He no longer worried about what anyone thought; they could go to hell if they tried to stop him.

*****

Bessie was also having a very enjoyable night. The

file she had found in Mr Cranky's office was a revelation. She was sure Lord Brandon had no idea this document still existed. She could understand why he'd kept it. The solicitor in him had taken precautions for exactly what was going to happen soon. This would really upset the apple cart.

The Return

18

Miles had left before Margot woke up the following morning, much to her relief. Now, in the cold light of day, thinking of what happened the previous night made her cringe with embarrassment.

That she had thrown herself willingly, with such wanton abandon, into the most amazing love making, was bad enough; but knowing she hadn't cared that Miles believed she was his beloved Meg was made worse by the fact she wanted more.

How can I face him and still act the way Meg would? How can I face Bessie, for that matter? She'll know immediately she sees me—and I won't have to say a word. And more importantly, how can I face myself?

Margot moaned and, grabbing her pillow from

under her head, covered her face with it and moaned again.

A tap at the door made her freeze. She lifted the pillow and stared at the door, willing it to stay shut. *Is it Miles? Please don't let it be him.*

When the door opened and Jane poked her head round, Margot gave a huge sigh, then smiled. 'Oh, Jane, I'm sorry, I'm not ready to get dressed yet. Can you give me ten minutes and then come back?'

Jane just nodded and closed the door again. Margot pulled back the covers and swung her legs over onto the floor. Putting the slippers on, she padded over to the decorative screen to use the commode, and then went to have a quick wash. How she missed her nice hot showers. She shivered, dipping the cloth into the bowl of cold water.

The next half hour was taken up with Jane helping her get prepared for the day ahead. She suddenly realised how hungry she was and couldn't wait to get down to the breakfast room.

After Jane had left, Margot was about to follow her, when Bessie walked into the room with a cheerful bounce in her step. She glanced past Margot to the tousled bed covers, and grinned.

'I's thinking you's either had a bad night, or a good one.'

Margot blushed and turned away. 'So how was your night? Was it productive?'

The Return

Bessie laughed aloud at Margot's immediate change of subject, but said no more about it. 'Yes, a very productive night. I's be telling you all about it after you've had your breakfast. I could smell it as I's passing the room.'

Suddenly food was forgotten. Instead, Margot was desperate to know what Bessie's search had revealed. 'Did you discover who will murder Meg?'

Bessie shook her head. 'No, I didn't. But I's thinking you'll be finding it very interesting, all the same. And I's knowing you'll be pleased. Now, go and get something inside you before it gets cleared away. Then I'll tell you all about it.'

Margot decided it would be pointless trying to argue. So, saying she wouldn't be long, she left Bessie in the room and went to have her breakfast. The delicious smells that greeted her as she walked into the room were enticing, and Margot's stomach rumbled, reminding her how hungry she was.

The food was being kept warm in dishes placed on hot trays, heated by small, dumpy candles. She chose kedgeree, followed by two slices of freshly made bread, butter and homemade jam. On the table was a big pot of tea, the milk in a smaller jug by the side.

It wasn't long before Margot began to unwind. She finished her plate of food, and poured herself a cup of tea. It was only then she saw the note. Curious, she picked it up. It was addressed to Meg. Margot frowned, and taking a knife, she slit the envelope and removed the letter.

After she'd read it, an equal measure of relief and disappointment rushed through her. Miles had received a message calling him to London. There was no way he could get out of it because it was of the utmost importance that he attends. He'd be gone a few days but would send a note if he was going to be longer.

A few days. That's good ... isn't it? Margot realised she'd been asking herself lots of questions of late, and hadn't been able to give herself a real answer, or a truthful one. *Was it good, or, was it bad? Of course, it's good. It leaves me free to help Bessie. Yes, it's good.*

She quickly drained her cup, then dashed up the stairs to her room to give Bessie her news. 'This means we'll have plenty of time to continue with our investigations without any interruptions,' she said, with as much gaiety as she could muster. 'So, what have you got to tell me?'

Bessie put her hand inside her deep pocket and brought out some documents. 'I's decided to bring them all with me this time,' she said, unfolding and spreading the papers out on the bed. 'Have a read of this one. You's going to have the biggest shock of your life.'

Margot took the document from Bessie and leaned

against the bed's footboard to read it. Her eyes widened as she skimmed over the document, then glanced up at Bessie. 'Phew. This is dynamite.' She picked up the next two and went over to sit at the table by the window.

The letter was from Lord Brandon to Mr Crankston-Smythe detailing their scheme and asking the solicitor to proceed with it immediately.

'Meg's father was set up. It was all arranged that they bankrupt him by getting him to invest in a company that didn't exist.' Margot couldn't believe what she was reading. 'Why would Lord Brandon do such a thing? And how on earth did Lord Crawford fall for such a plan? Didn't he take advice?'

'He thought he had,' Bessie replied. 'Don't forget Mr Crankston-Smythe was his solicitor, too.' She nodded her head towards the next documents on the bed.

'If'n you read that next one, you'll see that Lord Brandon didn't consider Lord Crawford rich enough for his son to marry Meg. There were more influential and well-off families with young daughters who would be more than willing and very available to marry Miles,' Bessie told her.

'It must have been obvious to Lord Brandon that Miles wasn't bothered about the financial side of the marriage, he just wanted to marry Meg. See this letter here?'

She picked up the other documents and took them over to the table, holding one out to Margot. 'It really drops him in the muck, and when it all comes out … which it's going to, old Cranky has covered himself with this unwittingly written confession from Miles' father.'

Margot took the document that was being held out for her and read it while Bessie waited.

'This is awful, Bessie. Lord Crawford certainly fell for Lord Brandon's lies, and you can't blame him when it was backed up by his own solicitor.' Margot stared down at the paper, shaking her head. 'But what happened to Lord Crawford's money?'

Bessie shrugged. 'I's thinking Lord Brandon and Mr Crankston-Smythe shared it. I's not finding anything to say it went anywhere else.'

'Miles will go ballistic,' Margot said. 'That his father ruined Lord Crawford
financially and his good name, just to stop him marrying Meg … well it's criminal. I'm going to hate telling Miles. Hang on, how can I show him? He'll wonder how I came to have them. This has to be thought out more.'

'I's been thinking on that, too.' Bessie stared with vacant eyes at the document Margot was holding in her hands. 'There might be a way … But I's going to have to wait until Miles is at home, and Lord Brandon isn't.'

The Return

Margot watched Bessie's ever-changing expressions as she continued to think. 'Well? What's your idea?' she prompted.

'When such a time comes, I's thinking we will put the documents in an envelope. I'll put Miles' name on it. He won't know my handwriting, and when I know the butler isn't around, I'll drop it in their entrance hall by the front door. That way, when the butler comes back, he will see it and deliver it to Miles.'

'Hmm, that sounds like a plan. He won't know who delivered it, and will be too curious not to open it.' Margot smiled and nodded. 'Yes, I think that's an excellent plan. Well done.'

'Now I's wanting to get my hands on the suicide note that the crooked solicitor read out to the family. *And* I's be needing something written by old Cranky to compare the handwriting.'

'I think I might have another suggestion that would serve just as well. If I can find a letter that Meg's father has written so we can compare it with the writing on the note, then, if it *is* different, we'll have all the evidence we need. I'll look in the study and search the files that Lady Crawford managed to bring along with her. I'm hoping she might have kept a private letter from him.'

'I's not thinking of that. That'd be good. But I's still going to search for something with Cranky's writing on it, as well as the suicide note. I'll go back

Sandra Stoner-Mitchell

while you're asleep tonight. I's pinched a bunch of keys that looked like a spare set. One fits the main door. I's checked it out already,' she told Margot with a satisfied grin.

'We might as well start our search for Lord Crawford's handwriting. You can't do anything else until late tonight.' Margot rose and led the way down to the study.

The search was proving fruitless until Bessie opened a book of household accounts. It was nothing to do with what they were looking for, but a loose piece of paper slipped out onto the floor.

Bessie picked it up and, after reading it, smiled. 'This'll do us nicely.'

19

'What? What have you found?' Margot dropped what she was looking at, and went across to Bessie, who was standing, rereading the letter she'd found.

'I's thinking this is the real suicide note that Lord Crawford left. Lady Crawford was the first on the scene after he'd shot his self, and she must have picked it up. You's going to be a mite upset'

Margot took the letter from Bessie and sat on one of the chairs to read it aloud.

'My dearest Emma,
When you find this, I will already be gone. I pray to God that one day you will find it in your heart to forgive me. I know this is the coward's way out, but I could not bear to see the love driven from your eyes and be replaced with disappointment.

Sandra Stoner-Mitchell

All I have left to give is advice. Please heed my words, my darling. Don't trust what others tell you. Especially those you believe are your friends. They will stab you in the back.

I leave you in the hope that compassion will prevail; and those who deliberately cheated me with lies and false promises, will make sure you will be properly taken care of.

I die a broken man at having to write this to you. Please forgive me.

Your devoted husband.

Charles.'

Margot stared at the letter for a moment before looking at Bessie. 'The poor man. If only he'd written down the way he'd been cheated. Unfortunately, Lord Crawford hasn't even mentioned their names. He could be talking about anyone. But *we* know who is responsible, and hopefully, everyone else will soon.

'At least I can show Miles *this* note. It's enough to back up what these documents have revealed. Perhaps I should hold on to this until we know he's seen them. What do you think?'

Bessie took the note back and stared at it. 'Hmm, I's not knowing if that would be such a good idea. If'n you show it to Miles now he won't know what it means anyway. But, when he gets to see these other documents, it will all fall into place. On its own, it could mean that he were cheated out of his money by the people he played cards with. It's only us that knows the truth. Meg wouldn't, and if'n it were her showing him this note, it would be done in all innocence.'

They both fell silent for a moment. Margot pulled her hair to the front of her shoulder and with slow, absentminded movements, twisted a lock through her fingers.

'I wonder if Lord Crawford even *knew* that Lord Brandon, and that sleazy solicitor, were going to tell everyone he'd lost his money gambling. Somehow, I don't think he did.' Her eyes dropped to the letter Bessie was still holding. 'You're right. I'll show it to Miles when he comes back and ask him what he thinks it means. That should cover it.'

The following days saw Margot looking for anything else that could help their cause. Going up to search the attic, she was taken aback at how little there was up there. A lot less than when she searched the attic in her own time.

Of course it's emptier, you dolt. All of what's up here in my time, is either still in use, or hasn't been bought yet.

Turning to retrace her steps down the stairs, she reached the attic door, then stopped. She looked back at the boxes. *But there might be other things here that I've not seen yet.*

On that thought, she searched around, but still only came away with her hair covered in cobwebs. Thoroughly fed-up, she descended the stairs to continue her search in the study and was still there when Bessie came back with a triumphant smile on her face.

'How come you always find something and I don't?' Margot flopped down on the chair, totally irritated. 'Okay, what have you found this time?'

Bessie was shaking her head. 'You's found the suicide note. So stop acting like a big kid, and I's be showing you what I's got.'

Margot's lips twitched as she tried to look suitably chastened. 'Sorry. But I've found nothing, only dust and cobwebs in the attic. So, what you've got?

They both went to sit at the desk where Bessie could display her treasure. First out was the fake will, followed by a copy of Mr Crankston-Smythe's handwriting. She'd decided to bring them back to show Margot.

'Let's get closer to the window. The light in here is abysmal without lighting all the candles.

Margot moved over and held both letters up to the light. 'Look at the letter Y in, Your devoted husband, and now look at the Y in the fake suicide note. They are nothing alike. But compare the fake note to the Y in this other piece the solicitor has written on, and they're identical. The rest of the writing is also quite different to Lord Crawford's handwriting.'

After they were both satisfied that Lord Crawford hadn't written the fake note, they congratulated themselves on doing some incredible detective work.

'I think we have all the proof we need. Now to present it to Miles.' Margot could not have been more delighted if she'd won the lottery.

'Let's see if there's an envelope big enough to put these, and the other documents into. Then they'll be ready for when I's taking them over to the big house.'

There wasn't, but they found some sealing wax, and sheets of brown paper to wrap them in. Bessie prepared the wax while Margot wrapped the documents ready to be sealed.

*****

After Jane had helped her out of her cage and corset, Margot sent her and the cook home. Now she was sitting in the kitchen drinking a cup of coffee while Bessie sat and watched.

'How you can drink that muck, I's not knowing. If only we could've brought yours back with us.' Bessie put her elbows on the table, supporting her chin on her interlaced fingers. Her thoughts went back to the coffee she'd tasted in the future, and released a wistful sigh.

Margot chuckled and put the cup on the table. 'I

have to admit, it's not a patch on Nescafé. It's much too bitter for me. Perhaps I'll stick with tea while I'm here. That's not too bad.'

'I's been thinking. It's yours and Meg's birthday in two days. I's wondering if Miles'll be back in time.'

'I can't see him missing it. Not if the vivid vision I had when I was opening the trunks in my time was true. I remember seeing Meg in Miles arms, dancing. She was wearing a lovely emerald-green ball gown that complemented her hair. I thought it was me back then, but now I know differently.'

'Hmm, I's thinking it *were* you. You's not finished here, yet.'

'Yes, you could be right. But it was a big party with many people there. Who would come? She doesn't seem to have any friends.'

This time, Bessie didn't answer. She appeared to be as much in the dark as Margot.

*****

Richard was already seated when Gwendolyn walked into the dining room. He stood up and went around the table to hold the chair out for her.

'You look happy tonight, my dear,' he told her as he went back to his own chair. 'It's obvious something happened to improve your mood. Are you going to share it?'

The Return

Gwendolyn could barely contain herself. She ignored his sarcasm; he couldn't dampen her happiness tonight.

She waited until the butler had placed her napkin on her lap, and poured her a glass of wine. Richards was already poured. Gwendolyn took a sip before speaking. She wanted to keep him waiting, but it was killing her.

The news her maid had given her while she was being helped into her gown had been the best she'd heard in a very long time. She knew it would upset Richard—which was the best part.

'Yes, I received news that might be of interest to you, my dear husband.' She took another sip of wine then put the glass back on the table. 'It seems Miles is holding a surprise party for your sister. You *do* remember her, don't you? It's her birthday in two days.' Watching the blood drain from Richard's eyes, and his hands knuckle into fists, was exactly what she was hoping for.

'And you know this … How?'

Gwendolyn kept her smile as bright as she could, even though the vitriol in his voice had frightened her somewhat.

'Oh, you know how servants talk, dear. It seems that Miles has sent invites to some of his closest friends. It is to be a surprise for Meg's birthday. From what I understand, Miles and Meg are still very much together, and there might be a wedding in the not-too-distant future.'

Richard's reaction wasn't quite what Gwendolyn had expected. Angry, yes, furious, absolutely, but the man who sat opposite her, she no longer knew.

Her gaze roamed unwillingly over his contorted, crazed features; his clenched jaw, his flared nostrils, and up to his eyes. They locked; she couldn't pull away. Only minutes before they'd been cool and indifferent. Now hard and cold, they narrowed into insane, murderous slits.

In Gwendolyn's mind, he seemed to expand as his rage heightened. She shrank back into her chair; she'd never been so frightened, yet her smile remained frozen in place. Richard pushed away from the table, sending the chair toppling to the floor. He stared at his wife; his face twisted with all the pent up hate he'd harboured for her for years.

'That is not going to happen, so you can wipe that supercilious smile off your ugly face.' And with that, he marched out of the room, slamming the door behind him.

Gwendolyn lifted her glass with a shaking hand. She gazed at the upturned chair and hiccuped a stifled giggle. Then, unable to stop herself, she laughed, hysterical, unnatural laughter, until tears of abject misery ran down her face. The satisfaction she'd expected to feel, had not happened.

The Return

20

There was a jaunty bounce in Miles' step as he left the Palace of Westminster; anyone seeing his smile, which also added a sparkle to his eyes, would not be wrong in thinking him to be exceedingly pleased with himself.

The surprise at winning the vote in the House of Lords for reforms to improve the lives of the poor and vulnerable, a subject Miles had been passionate about for years, had quite bowled him over.

He now headed across Westminster to see his best friend, Joshua Fellows. It wasn't far, and as it was a nice day, he decided to walk. Joshua was at home and greeted his friend with a warm smile and a firm handshake. After the butler had left the room and closed the door, Joshua indicated one of the chairs.

I thought you might be here for the vote, being one you've been badgering for these last couple of years. I can't think of anything else that could drag you away from the lovely Mistress Meg.' Joshua teased, pouring two glasses of port and taking them over to where Miles was sitting.

Miles took a sip and swirled it around his mouth, savouring the taste, before swallowing. He couldn't help the satisfied grin as he placed the glass on the coffee table in front of him.

'Actually, that wasn't the only reason I came up to the city. It just so happened the vote took place today, which, you'll be delighted to hear, passed with a huge majority,'

'That's excellent news. Congratulations. You worked hard to get that through. So, what was the other reason? Or is that ill-mannered of me to ask?'

Miles accepted the congratulations with a slight bow of the head. 'Thanks, Josh, and no, not ill-mannered at all, considering one of my other reasons concerns you. When I heard you were still in the city, I believed it to be a good omen and an opportune moment for me to come and ask yet another favour.'

Joshua's eyebrow lifted. 'Oh? Now I am intrigued. Fire away, then, and I'll see if I can help.' He sat back in his chair and crossed his legs, not once breaking eye contact.

'Well, you already know the main story, Josh, and

The Return

quite frankly, without you having my back all this time and helping to keep our secret, I'd have been out of my mind by now. These last nine years have caused Meg and myself a lot of misery, more so for Meg. I've had enough. The narrow-minded hypocrisy displayed by so-called upright citizens has worn me down. It's got to stop. I'm going to marry Meg at Christmas. What I want to know is, would you be my best man?'

Shock, followed immediately by immense pleasure, flashed across Joshua's face. 'And about bloody time. How often have I told you to forget the gossip mongers and marry the girl? Of course I'll be your best man, and proud that you've bestowed such an important role on me for your special day.'

He jumped up and, after pulling the cord for his butler, opened a cupboard in his drink's cabinet where he kept the humidor box filled with his favourite cigars, Casa Turrent's Claro Lancero.

'This calls for a celebration, my friend,' he said, bringing the box over and offering him one. 'This has to be the news of the century.'

Just at that moment, the butler opened the door and both men looked up. 'Ah, Robert, would you bring us a bottle of my finest champagne, please?'

'Certainly, Sir.'

Joshua, like the rest of society, had known about the scandal that had prevented his friend's marriage. It had been the juiciest gossip at every lady's tea-party for months—until the next scandal took its place. He'd tried for years to get his friend to forget convention and marry Meg. But Miles' mother had always lurked in the background.

For as long as he could remember, Miles had been warned of his mother's frail health. A firm reminder, that any shock would be likely to precipitate her death, had usually followed. He also remembered how quick his father had been to pick up on that when he told his son he could no longer allow his marriage to Meg. But Miles had recently discovered her to be a lot stronger than she'd have everyone believe.

After cutting and lighting their cigars, Joshua glanced over at his friend. 'So, what brought about the change of mind?'

'To be quite frank, I've simply had enough.' Miles dropped his eyes to his fingers, steepling on his lap. He sighed. 'I can't bear seeing Meg suffer as she does, Josh. Oh, she does a good job hiding it, but I know what she's going through. It's not fair on her to be subjected to this just because of what happened. It wasn't her fault, and we have more than enough money and status for that not to be a problem. Apart from that, I love her, and she loves me. Why should we have to sneak around like we do? No. I've had it up to here,' he said, raising his hand above his head. 'We will be married at Christmas. My parents can come if they want. It will be their choice; I don't care either way.'

'Well said. Bravo. You have my total support, my friend. Ah, here's Robert with the champagne.' They both watched as the butler filled the flutes and handed one to each of the men. Joshua lifted his glass, 'Cheers.'

After they'd both taken a sip, they spoke of where the wedding reception would be held. While they were together, they also discussed Meg's surprise party, which Joshua confirmed was all organised at his mansion. His wife, Sarah, was overseeing the event and had sworn their servants to secrecy. Joshua would be travelling back that day and expected to be home later the following afternoon.

'Speaking of which, I have to go and collect Meg's dress. That was the other reason I came up to the city. I can't tell you how hard it is to buy a surprise gown for a lady. It's an experience I don't think I'll be having again. I was fortunate to find a model her size.'

Joshua laughed at the vision of his friend in a ladies' fashion room.

*****

Richard Crawford paced around his room, his mood getting more sinister by the moment. The idea that his sister would be marrying a relative of the King, no matter how distant, irked him more than words could describe. He had to stop it. How? *I'm her brother, Miles is supposed to come to me for permission to marry her now my coward of a father isn't around.*

He stopped pacing as another thought came to him, one that just might work to stop the wedding. *If I didn't know about it, being her brother, then I'm sure Lord Brandon doesn't either. There has to be a way to put him in the picture.*

Therein lay the problem. Without admitting it, Richard was more of a coward than his father. The idea of approaching Lord Brandon filled him with dread. The way the older man held himself, sniffed, raised his head and stared down his nose at him, made Richard feel less than one of his servants. He'd endured the humiliation every time he'd had the misfortune to bump into him.

Richard started pacing again, eyes down and his hand rubbing the short neat beard while he thought of a way to do this. *I need to talk to someone who bears Miles a grudge. But who?*

The more he thought, the more he realised no one in their right mind would stand up to Lord Brandon. And even a friend wouldn't relish the idea of delivering the news of his son's continued relationship with Meg. It was becoming all too obvious this was not something he could get someone else to do. He'd have to contrive a way to orchestrate it—causing the least harm to himself.

The Return

Down in the kitchen, Jenkins, Gwendolyn's butler, had kept away from the dining room until he was called. This was not unusual in situations of this kind. His sympathies, of course, were with his mistress. He'd known her since she was a young girl, having been her father's butler as well. Quite frankly, he would have left had it not been for Gwendolyn. She needed an ally, and he was it.

That he'd disliked Mr Turnbull, was no secret, at least, not between the two of them. Jenkins had always regarded her father as just a commoner, like the rest of the staff. But he'd made money, which had given him airs and graces way above his station. That was his personal opinion. Then Gwendolyn was forced to marry an equally obnoxious man, who treated her with the same abysmal disregard. Having been brought up to respect women, it had appalled Jenkins to see the way these two treated her.

Now the bell in the kitchen tinkled. Jenkins instructed the serving girl to follow him with her ladyship's meal. The routine on such an occasion never varied. There would be no formal service, Lady Crawford would only eat a small meal. It happened far too often for his liking.

Walking into the dining room, he was struck by the look of defeat in her eyes. This was not good. After the maid had placed her ladyship's plate in front of her, and bobbed a curtsy, she left the room.

Jenkins moved up to the table and, picking up the bottle of wine, he topped up Gwendolyn's glass. She looked up and gave a feeble smile.

'I believe the time has come for me to arrange the *special* meal for his lordship, Madam. I believe Cook has most of the ingredients in the pantry. I can soon get the other one.'

Gwendolyn held her glass mid-way to her mouth, then lowered her arm. She turned to face him. He raised a brow. A smile tugged at her lips.

'I think that would be a marvellous idea. How about something rich and spicy, you know how much Lord Crawford enjoys those, just like my late father did. That special ingredient I found by chance, growing in the garden, does add that little extra kick, don't you think?'

Her smile deepened. 'Thank you, Jenkins. You always know how to bring me out of the doldrums. Suddenly, I feel quite hungry.'

The Return

21

Miles turned up at Margot's home carrying a large box. It was mid-afternoon, and already the October nights were closing in. The drawing room door was open, and Miles stood for a moment watching her. A warmth flooded his senses as he gazed with more love than he thought possible for one man to feel. That Margot hadn't heard him enter, was obvious by the concentration etched on her face as she read the letter in her hand. When she *did* look up, she gave a startled gasp.

'I didn't realise you were back from London, Miles. How did it go?' She quickly tucked the letter away in her pocket and stood up. 'It sounded important from the note you left me. Is everything all right?'

Miles chuckled, putting the box on the sofa. 'So

many questions. Yes, it was all good. You remember the bill I've been trying to get approved in Parliament? Well, it passed by a huge majority.' He went over and, lifting her up, he kissed her as if he hadn't seen her in weeks instead of the few days he'd been away.

Standing beside the widow, invisible to Miles, Bessie explained to Margot what the bill was about. 'I's knowing it made a big difference in the future. Now, don't you go'n forget the letter. Yous got plenty of time for all that nibbling after he's read it.' Bessie couldn't help laughing at her own little quip.

'That's marvellous news, Miles. Congratulations. I'm so proud of you,' she told him once he'd released her lips. Her delight in his achievement was genuine; she couldn't be more pleased for him.

'Thank you, Meg.' He pulled her into his arms again and inhaled her delicate perfume. Then held her away so he could gaze into her eyes. 'I missed you.'

'I missed you, too, Miles.' This was no lie. Margot *had* missed him … too much.

'I've recently been thinking a lot about the way we've been forced to live our lives, and I don't like it. I know you don't either—No, let me finish.' He touched her lips with his finger when she opened her mouth to speak. 'It's no good denying it. I know how sad you've been since your mother died, and now you are on your own here, it's made it even worse.'

The Return

Margot gently pulled his finger away. 'So long as I have you, I'm content, Miles. Truly.'

He smiled and stroked her cheek. 'I once thought that would be enough, my sweet Meg, but it's not. And I'm damned if I'm going to sit back and let others dictate how we live our lives. Because of that, I've come to a decision, we are going to start meeting other people as a betrothed couple again.

'While I was in Westminster, I called on Josh, seeing as he was at his townhouse nearby. He knows my feelings, and suggested a good start would be a double celebration to celebrate your birthday and the bill being passed. He has arranged a dinner party at his mansion tomorrow night. It was to be a surprise, but on my way home, I thought you'd appreciate some warning so you could prepare yourself.'

Margot stared into Miles' sparkling eyes, and couldn't help smiling. Although she already knew about the surprise party, she had to keep up the pretence. 'But, Miles, what about your family? They will be furious.'

'Don't you fret, my sweet one. All will be taken care of. Now, you haven't asked me yet what I have in the box I brought in with me. That's most unusual for a lady.'

Margot leaned sideways in order to look past Miles and see the box. She glanced at it, and back to Miles.

'Okay, what have you been buying in London?'

Sandra Stoner-Mitchell

'Open the box and find out,' he told her.

She hesitated, already having an idea what it contained. *The ball gown I saw in the trunk isn't anywhere in the house yet, so this could be it.*

Going over to the box, she carefully began removing the paper. She could see Miles' hand out the corner of her eye, edging forward to help, then pulling back.

With the paper out the way, she lifted the top, and stared. The gown looked even more beautiful than it did when she saw it all those years in the future. Her hands reached out to pick the gown up by the top of the little sleeves.

'Oh, Miles. It's beautiful. I love emerald green, it's my favourite colour; and the sequins in the bodice...' Margot looked up into Miles' eyes. 'I love it, Miles, thank you.'

Margot held it close to her, to let Miles see how it looked. 'What do you think?' she asked, as a sudden shyness crept over her.

'I'd love you in whatever you wore, my sweet. Will you wear it for tomorrow's celebration? You'll look stunning. I'll be the envy of every man there.'

'I will. But now, I must go and hang the gown up before it creases.'

'And I'll bring the rest.' Miles went to collect the other gifts that were still in the box.

'The rest? There's more? Oh, Miles, you shouldn't

169

The Return

keep spoiling me this way.' Margot could feel the tears welling. *If only this was for me; if only it was me he loved...*

'You go ahead and I'll follow with these.'

Once in the spare room, which she used as a walk-in wardrobe, Margot hung up the gown. Now, as she stood back to admire it, she sighed. 'If only...'

'If only, what, my sweet?' Miles came and stood in front of her and, putting a finger under her chin, tilted her face up to look at him. 'If only, what?' He encouraged.

Margot cursed herself for speaking aloud. 'Oh, it's just that it's so beautiful, I wish the celebration was tonight.'

Miles laughed. 'You had me worried for a moment. Tomorrow will come soon enough. Here, open these two boxes.' He placed them on the bed and stood back to watch.

One box contained a pair of exquisite, emerald-green, satin dance shoes and the other a matching full-length, fur-trimmed, hooded cape. Margot had not expected these, not having seen them in the attic in her time.

Miles took the cape and told her to turn around so that he could put it over her shoulders. A full-length mirror stood in the corner of the room and Margot went over to see how the cape looked on her.

'It's so lovely, Miles,' she whispered. 'Thank

you.' She couldn't help herself; she wanted a hug. She stood on tiptoe so her arms reached up and her fingers linked together around the back of his neck.

That was all Miles needed. With one motion, he'd whipped the cape from her shoulders, lifted her into his arms, and carried her over to the bed.

'I's thinking she's forgotten all about the letter.' Bessie made her way back down the stairs, shaking her head.

*****

Richard Crawford walked into the Gentlemen's Club and, standing at the bottom of the stairs leading to the bar, he took a deep breath. This would be his only chance. He knew Lord Brandon would be there, being Friday, and the evening when titled gentlemen came together before the weekend set in.

His stomach had given him some painful cramps this evening; he'd put them down to nerves. Another caught him as he stood there. *Get a hold of yourself, for crying out loud. You've got to do this.*

He took a handkerchief from his pocket and wiped the sweat from his brow. Then lifting his chin, Richard straightened his necktie, flicked some imaginary flecks from his jacket, then marched with determination up to the bar. His heart thumped painfully, but he wouldn't turn back now.

As usual, the bar was packed. He didn't need to

The Return

look to know where Lord Brandon sat; his booming, pompous voice travelled the room, decibels above all the others.

Richard edged his way over to a table where two people were sitting chatting. He knew them both well—that they hadn't turned their backs on him, like some he could mention, was a stroke of luck.

He deliberately pretended not to see Lord Brandon even though he could feel his eyes burning the back of his head. Reaching his target and, needing support, he held onto the back of an empty seat. For some unknown reason, his arms were beginning to numb, as if he no longer owned them. He felt clammy. *For heaven's sake, he can't kill you, not in front of all these witnesses. Get a grip. You're nearly there.*

'Good evening, gentlemen, would you mind if I joined you?' he asked brightly.

Lord Bailey and Baron Hill, nodded and Richard pulled out the chair. He gave a loud sigh as he sat, pulling the chair closer to the table.

'I had to come and clear my head before I travel home,' he told them. When the waiter came to the table, Richard ordered a large brandy, then turned to his companions. 'Gentlemen, can I get you anything?'

Both declined, having only just had their glasses refilled. 'You seem to be a bit down, Lord Crawford,' Baron Hill said. 'I trust Lady Crawford is in good health?'

'Pardon? Oh, I'm sorry. I suppose a bit down, is a good way of putting my feelings at the moment. Lady Crawford is well, thank you for asking. No, I've just heard some disturbing news.' The waiter came back and Richard took the opportunity to surreptitiously see if Lord Brandon was listening.

After the waiter had left them, Richard continued. 'I've just learnt that my *dear* sister, Meg, is still with Miles Brandon. Apparently, they've never been apart, and he's putting on a grand party for her birthday tomorrow. I feel rather hurt that I wasn't invited. I mean, you'd think your own blood relation would at least be told.'

'Excuse me for intruding, Lord Crawford, but I couldn't help overhearing your conversation. I believe you mentioned my son's name. Would you like to repeat your slanderous remarks to me, Sir?' He spat out the words as his puffed-out cheeks turned the same colour as his purple bulbous nose.

The room quieted; everyone wanted to hear what would happen next. For some reason, Richard didn't feel the slightest bit in awe of the man towering above him. Instead, he forced his leaden arm to move, pick up his glass, and take a sip.

'I don't think anyone can call the truth, slander, Lord Brandon. If you don't believe me, ask your son. I've also heard that a wedding might not be too far in the future.'

The Return

Before he could put his glass back on the table, Lord Brandon grabbed the front of Richard's shirt, and pulled him out of his chair, causing Richard's brandy to splash down his shirt.

Lord Brandon's friends leapt from their seats to pull him away from Richard. 'Leave it. We all know it's a lie,' one of them said, turning to look at the people around him. Many shifted in their seats and, keeping their heads lowered, deliberately avoided eye contact.

Lord Brandon stiffened. Understanding for the first time that his son had disobeyed him. He let go of Richard, who fell back against the table.

'So, how many of you knew of this? Or don't any of you lily-livered, spineless idiots have the guts to tell me?' Lord Brandon's eyes scoured the men. When no one answered, his eyes filled with such contempt, anyone having the nerve to face him, visibly shrivelled under his gaze.

His face fused with anger, and, pushing the men aside who were standing in his way, stormed out of the room.

The silence that followed was shattered when the bar steward dropped the tray of drinks he'd been holding. The men who had Miles' confidence, gave Richard a look that told him just what they thought of him.

Not that it bothered him one iota. He'd done what

he'd set out to do. Now all he had to do was sit and wait for the fireworks to explode. His heart chose that moment to give him a vicious, painful kick. He groaned and doubled over, falling
to the floor, now gasping for air…

The last thing Richard remembered before losing consciousness was his wife, Gwendolyn's, face. He remembered thinking how strange it was to see her actually smiling at him at the dinner table. It hadn't registered at the time—It did now.

'You ~~ freaking ~~ murderi—'

22

It wasn't until the following morning, when Margot was leaving her room to go for breakfast, that she remembered the letter. She quickly retrieved it and took it with her.

Miles was already at the table, pouring himself a cup of coffee. He stood up when Margot came into the room.

'Happy Birthday, darling. How is the love of my life feeling this morning?' He left the table and went straight to her. 'I have to say, a more radiant smile I've yet to see.' He wrapped his arms around her and bent to kiss her before she had a chance to say anything.

Margot surrendered to his kisses, realising she only had two weeks left to stop Meg's murder and two weeks left with Miles. That thought made her shiver.

'Are you cold?' Miles placed his hands on her shoulders and stood away to look into her eyes.

'No, not cold. Nervous,' she fibbed. 'I feel like a child being taken to see the head-teacher; only tonight there will be many head-teachers to face.'

'There is nothing to worry about. They are all friends, and anyway, I'll be by your side for the whole evening.' Miles led her over to the table, pulling out a chair for her to sit on and have her breakfast.

They ate in silence, both locked in their own thoughts. It wasn't until they were enjoying their second cup of coffee that Margot brought the letter out of her pocket.

'This fell out of a book I picked up, Miles, but I don't understand what it means. Would you take a look, please?'

Miles took the letter from her outstretched hand. A deep frown creased his brow, almost causing his eyebrows to touch. He spent a few minutes studying the
wording while Margot watched and waited.

When he handed the letter back, he looked baffled. He brought his elbows up to the table, and rested his chin on his knuckles. The frown remained in place as he continued to think. 'You say it fell out of a book?'

'Yes. I was looking for something to read while you were away. It's very strange wording, don't you think? It's certainly nothing like the one the solicitor read out. In fact, I don't remember him even showing it to us, or the will.'

Miles picked up his cup and drained it. 'That is strange. I think it might be a good idea if I go and see our Mr Crankston-Smythe. I'd like to have a look at the will, and that letter he read out. Something doesn't sound right.'

Bessie, sitting on the table with her feet resting on one of the chairs, was frantically shaking her head. 'No. He can't do that. You's gotta stop him.'

Margot tried to suppress a smile and lowered her head, concentrating instead on folding the letter and putting it back in her pocket. When she looked up, she'd managed to compose herself again.

'Can we forget about it for now, Miles? Tonight is going to be a wonderful evening to celebrate your win in Parliament, and showing the world we are together. I don't want to risk anything going wrong and spoiling it.'

Miles smiled. Pushing his plate aside, he reached across the table and held her hand. 'You're right. I won't do anything yet. It's not as if there's any urgency. We'll deal with it after the party.'

*****

Miles was in a jovial mood when he arrived back home. Now he'd started taking back his life, with decisions made and implemented, he couldn't wait to show Meg off at her party. Many of his friends would be there; only those out of the country couldn't make it.

He'd planned to go straight to his room and freshen up before going over to see Joshua. He wanted to check all was in place for the party, but was side-lined by his father. Miles didn't much like the look on his face.

'Good evening, Father. I was just going up to my room. Is there something on your mind?'

'Damned right there's something on my mind. Get in here.' Lord Brandon snarled, shutting the door behind them. 'I'll get straight to the point, Miles, I have just been outrageously humiliated in the gentlemen's club by that rapscallion, Crawford. And it's all down to you, sneaking around behind my back to see that woman after I explicitly forbade you to do so. What have you got to say for yourself?'

Miles was taken aback. He stared at his father's livid face and scowled, inwardly seething that Richard had somehow found out. 'I'm sorry you learned this way, Father, but yes, it's true. And, what's more, I will not give her up, nor will you stop me from marrying her. Now, if you'll excuse me, Father, I have a lot to do and I don't feel like standing here arguing. My mind is made up.'

'Your mind's made up? Your mind's made up?' he

said, screaming like a banshee. He spat the words, spittle spraying from his mouth and slobbering froth like a rabid dog. 'How dare you, Sir? How dare you speak to me like that? Let me tell you right now—you see that woman again, and you'll no longer be a son of mine. Do you hear me?'

Miles looked at his father and shook his head. 'Fine. Goodnight to you, Sir.' Miles turned and walked out of the room.

'Come back here right now. I've not finished with you yet.' Lord Brandon shouted, but Miles was already sprinting up the stairs to his room. He'd need to pack some clothes and take them with him to Joshua's.

*****

Joshua welcomed Miles into his mansion, and had the butler take his bags up to one of the many guest rooms. Ushering Miles into his study, he listened to his friend recount what had happened between him and his father, as he poured him a drink.

'Here,' He passed Miles his drink. 'So, do you have any idea how Lord Brandon found out?'

'No. I haven't the slightest idea. But when I do find out, I can assure you, that person will live to regret it.'

'I've also got news, Miles. Not good news … I received a note from Greg just after luncheon. He'll be here tonight, with his wife, by the way. It seems that after your father left the club last night, Lord Crawford keeled over and died. They are waiting for the results of a post-mortem. Apparently, he was clutching his heart as he collapsed. It could have been a heart-attack.'

Joshua looked down at his hands. Miles knew from this habit of his friend, that there was more. He waited.

'This is the weirdest part,' Joshua finally continued. 'Some of those standing closest to Lord Crawford said they heard him mention, "murder." In fact, two of them said it sounded very much like, "You murdering bitch." But how could that be possible? If he was referring to his wife, she wasn't even there.'

Miles ran his fingers through his hair, his frustration growing by the minute. Could anything else go wrong on Meg's birthday?

'Look, I hate putting on you like this, Josh, you are already doing more than I could possibly hope for.' He gave Josh a grateful look. 'But as the guests come, could you tell them not to mention any of this in front of Meg? In fact, not to mention it at all. Tell them I'll talk to them later.'

'Of course. Leave it to me. Now, I suggest you go up and get ready. You'll have to go and fetch Meg soon.'

The Return

Miles checked his pocket watch. 'Good heavens. Is it that time already? Thanks, Josh.' Miles rushed from the room and went to get ready.

*****

Jane finished putting the final touches to Margot's hair, then picked up the small hand mirror so she could see the back.

Margot turned her head one way and then another. Somehow, Jane had managed to tame her wild, red locks into a braided crown of glory, with tiny pearls clipped into each twist. The stunning effect was enhanced by a few ringlets falling onto her shoulders.

'You're an absolute miracle worker, Jane, I don't know how you've managed to turn my wild bush into this glorious work of art. Thank you.' Margot smiled at Jane who was standing by her side.

'I'm glad you like it, Mistress Meg.' She blushed a pretty pink as her face lit up with a smile.

Now it was time to step into her emerald-green ball gown. After Jane had finished, Margot turned to look into the full-length mirror. She'd never thought herself as being plain, but she'd never considered herself beautiful, either. However, the reflection staring back at her caused her jaw to drop. The off the shoulder gown, complete with her new hairstyle, left her astonished.

'Is that really me?' She twisted and turned, looking

at herself from all angles.

Jane smiled, pleased that she'd helped create the stunning lady standing in front of her. 'You'll be the belle of the ball, Mistress.'

'Thank you, Jane. It's all your doing, you know. Off you go. Tell Cook I said you can eat early and then go home. I'll be all right now.'

Jane bobbed a curtsy and left the room.

'I's thinking you's going to be turning some heads tonight,' Bessie told Margot. 'I's coming along, too. You don't know, we might learn something about Meg's murderer.'

'That's true. I never thought of that. Just so long as he or she doesn't try anything tonight. I don't think Miles would be too happy.' She turned and looked at herself in the mirror again. 'I can't believe that's me.'

Bessie smiled and, turning away, Margot barely heard her mutter, 'I's got a funny feeling in my stomach, that something is going to happen tonight.'

The Return

23

Margot heard Miles speaking to one of the maids as she was about to leave the bedroom, and swiftly stepped back into the room, closing the door and leaning against it.

'Miles is here already. This will be our last chance to chat together openly, so make sure you stay close by in case I need your help.'

Bessie nodded; her eyes devoid of their usual sparkle. 'You's got no need to fret. I's be watching you all the time—And, Margot ... be careful.'

Margot frowned, but a tap on the door meant there was no time left for discussion. It was Mavis, another maid, who came to tell her that Miles had arrived. Margot smoothed her skirts, looked at Bessie and whispered, 'Let's do this.'

She took a few steps forward, then stopped. 'My

cape. Mavis, would you fetch it for me, please, and bring it down with you?' Margot threw Bessie one last uneasy look, took a deep breath and left the room.

As she descended the stairs, Margot couldn't help feeling some pleasure at the look on Miles' face when he turned and saw her.

'Hello Miles, you look very handsome in your evening suit. You'll make me the envy of all the women at the party.' She meant it too. He did look rather dashing.

'I seriously doubt that. Have you any idea how gorgeous you look? Stunning doesn't quite cover it. You're an absolute vision. That all the women will be casting an envious eye in your direction, I will agree with. But you can be assured, it will have nothing to do with you being with me.'

Margot laughed. 'You do exaggerate somewhat, my dear Miles.'

She had reached the last step as Miles came to hold her hand. He brought it to his lips, then with one sudden movement, he held her in his arms.

'Good Lord, woman. What are you doing to me? You're a temptress. Come, we have to go or I might forget why I'm here.'

He released her and taking her cape from the maid, who was standing close by, put it around Margot's shoulders. Then, with a hand on her elbow, he steered her out the door to the waiting carriage. Margot waited a moment before getting in, giving Bessie a chance to slip in first, then she followed and made a point of spreading her skirts so that Miles wouldn't be sitting on Bessie's lap.

The ride was a short one, less than twenty minutes, and passed pleasantly with Miles explaining who would be there and that she was not to worry about anything. All those coming were happy for the pair of them. He hadn't told her that her best friend, Lucy Shivers, would be coming. He wanted that to be a surprise.

It was then that Margot realised she might be found out. She didn't have a clue who Miles was talking about.

'Don't worry,' Bessie told her, as if she had read Margot's mind. 'I's will be standing right behind you, whispering in your ear. You's gonna be fine.'

Miles had timed it so they would be at the mansion first. It was important that they stand together to greet their guests as they arrived.

Joshua and Sarah ushered Miles and Margot into their home, and had their butler take Margot's and Miles' outdoor clothing.

'Hello, Meg.' Sarah smiled and leant forward to kiss Margot's cheek. She linked arms and walked with her into her sitting room while Miles and Joshua discussed the evening ahead.

'It's been too long. I'm going to rectify that now

Miles has decided, at long last, to let the world know you are still a couple. How are you feeling? You look incredible.'

'Thank you, Sarah. But to be honest with you, I am *so* nervous. People can change a lot in nine years. What if I can't put a name to the face after all this time? And worse, what if they don't like me now and are only coming to please Miles?'

'I'd be surprised if you *weren't* nervous,' Sarah told her. 'You've isolated yourself for nearly a decade—and quite unnecessarily, in my opinion. I happen to know everyone coming tonight fully empathises with you. If they didn't, well, they probably wouldn't have wanted to come; and they *all,* without exception, did want to come.'

Sarah smiled and gave Margot a gentle hug. 'I promise you you'll forget all about being nervous once everyone is here.'

Miles chose that moment to walk into the room. 'Nervous? Who's nervous?'

'I am, Miles. But Sarah is right. Once I've met everyone again, I'll be fine.'

'Of course you will. You'll take it all in your stride, just like you do with everything,' he said, taking her hand and bringing it to his lips. 'What I came to tell you is, our guests are starting to arrive. Put that lovely smile on your face and we'll go and meet them.' He crooked his arm and tucked hers

The Return

inside, then, with gentle fingers, he stroked her hand. 'Ready then, my sweet, beautiful Meg?'

Margot couldn't help smiling back, and nodded. She glanced around and caught Bessie's eye.

'I's be right behind you.'

Taking a deep breath, Margot let Miles lead her to where they would greet their guests. Everything went well. Bessie whispered the guests' names as they came up, also adding little bits of information to help her. It was when a lovely young lady came up and stood in front of Margot, that she panicked a bit. It was as if the lady was waiting for something to happen.

Bessie was quick on the uptake. 'This is Lucy Shivers, Meg's best friend. Meg hasn't seen her since to the scandal broke.'

'Lucy. Oh, Lucy, how lovely to see you.' They fell into each other's arms, and laughed at being together again.

'I's thinking you belongs on the stage.' Bessie was impressed at how well Margot handled the situation.

Miles had been watching and congratulated himself on pulling off the surprise. There would be no more hiding away, regardless of his father's threat.

The evening soon got underway and all went well. Miles took Margot to the centre of the ballroom and led the first waltz. He privately enjoyed the glances directed at the lady in his arms.

Sandra Stoner-Mitchell

I chose the gown well. The emerald-green matches her eyes perfectly; and what a stunning effect it is paired with her glorious red hair. I'll be hard-pressed keeping myself under control tonight.

Margot kept her eyes on Bessie and, true to her word, she stayed close by. She'd occasionally say something, explain a memory of one of the guests so Margot would know how to respond. Through the evening, Margot tried to memorise who was who. She knew if she forgot, Bessie would be quick to remind her, but it would be better if she could be spontaneous.

The evening was into its third hour when a ruckus could be heard outside. Moments later the ballroom doors were pushed open, and there stood a drunk, enraged, very loud, Lord Brandon.

The orchestra stopped playing and everyone stood rooted to the spot. The quietness was unsettling, more so when Miles walked up and stood in front of his father.

'You are very welcome to stay, Father, if you have come to tell me that you've finally come to your senses and will welcome Meg into the family.'

Lord Brandon looked around the room, and sneered. 'Come to my senses? I've come to see the traitors in this room.' He pointedly stared at those nearest to him. 'I'll remember you all.' Then he turned and his eyes fell on Margot.

He walked, albeit unsteadily, up to her. 'As for

The Return

you, Madam. You will never get your hands on my money. I know exactly what you are … you … you're just like your greedy father, out for all you can—'

'I think you've said enough, Sir, now you can leave.' Miles, none too gently, took hold of his father's arm and forced him out of the room.

'Let go of me. How dare you treat me like the scum you mix with.'

Miles struggled to control his temper. He had half a mind to punch his father. 'Let me tell you, Sir, if you weren't my father, you'd be lying on the floor with a bloody nose.' He clenched his fists and thrust them in his pocket. 'If you ever speak to the lady I intend to marry like that again, I will not be responsible for my actions. So, you can thank your lucky stars, I, at least, have some manners.'

The more Lord Brandon struggled and ranted; the more aggressive Miles became. When he finally managed to get his father outside, he called the coachman down to help put him into the carriage.

'I suggest you go home and try to sober up. You disgraced yourself tonight, Father. You owe Meg an apology, and many others here, too.' He slammed the carriage door and let the coachman know Lord Brandon was ready to leave.

Without another word, Miles stood back and watched the coach turn and move away. Now he had some apologies to make on his father's behalf. *What a lovely evening this has turned out to be.*

But something niggled, his father was so determined to stop his marriage to Meg. Why? Miles' thoughts travelled to the letter. It wasn't the words of a gambler. The more he thought about it, and his father's behaviour…

The Return

24

After watching the carriage drive off, Miles stood for a while gathering his thoughts, wondering what he should do next. Realising now that his father was up to something, he wanted to know what, and why. His good friends had been insulted by his father. He had no idea how Meg must be feeling.

For now, I have to bide my time. Until then, I've got to make my father see what his disgraceful behaviour is doing to the family ... But how? How the hell can I stop an arrogant, odious....

Miles shook his head. Name calling wasn't helping. He took a deep breath and headed back inside, bracing himself for the anger he was expecting, and to apologise to his friends and his sweet Meg. Instead, when he walked into the ballroom he froze; totally bemused, unable to register the astonishing sight in front of him.

Everything seemed to be the way it was before his father had burst in. The music had started again and a few guests were dancing. Others were standing around with a glass in their hand, talking as if nothing untoward had happened. To say he was surprised would be an understatement.

Joshua came up to him with two glasses in his hand. He passed one to Miles. 'The best whisky in my cellar. Cheers.'

Miles took the glass and almost downed the fiery liquid in one large swig.

'What the hell happened? When I escorted Father out to his carriage, I thought I'd return to find everyone getting their belongings together and leaving as fast as they could.'

'Ah, but you didn't know then what a remarkable future wife you have. I wish you'd seen her. She went to the front of the room, standing by the orchestra, and apologised in the most charming, genteel way to everyone here. She said they mustn't take anything that Lord Brandon said personally, because it wasn't about them, it was about her. She went on to say it would be nice if they would stay for *your* sake.' Joshua grinned.

'You should see your face, Miles. Meg also said she was grateful to everyone who had come tonight to help with her return into society. I've never seen anything like it. Everyone applauded her. She was magnificent.'

'Meg said all that?' Miles was filled with a mixture of pride, amazement, and overwhelming love.

'Yes. Every word. After tonight, there'll not be a person around who won't want to invite her into their homes. She has certainly gained everyone's respect and admiration this evening.'

Miles looked around, searching for his Meg. He smiled when he saw her engaged in lively conversation with Sarah and, excusing himself, went over to join them.

'Miles. Is your father alright? I was worried he'd hurt himself.' Her eyes showed her concern was genuine.

'Can you believe this woman, Sarah? After what my father said, and worse, what he and my mother have put her through all these years, she's worried about *him*?' Miles scratched his head, quite bewildered. He then turned to Meg saying 'He's not good enough to even walk in your shadow.'

He reached out and held her hands. 'I've sent him home in his carriage. Hopefully, he'll have a sore head in the morning as well and remember what he did here tonight. Now my dear, sweet Meg, if Sarah won't mind me stealing you away, I'd like to ask if you would do me the greatest honour of having the next dance with me?'

Sarah smiled. 'I'm sure Meg would rather dance with you, than stand here chatting to me. Go ahead, I have to check on the refreshments.' She leaned over and kissed Margot on the cheek. 'Well done. What you did tonight took a great deal of courage.'

When the waltz was announced, Miles led Margot on to the dance floor. He pulled her close, and whispered, 'You never cease to amaze me. Are you *really* okay? My father was particularly obnoxious tonight.'

The music began to play before Margot had a chance to reply. She took a few moments, delighting in the way he held her and, with skilled movements, led her around the floor. When she looked up, her eyes were sparkling. 'Nothing, and definitely not Lord Brandon, is going to ruin tonight for me. If I worried about it, and scurried back home, he would have won.'

'Good for you. Do you know how much I love you?'

Margot nodded, wishing more than ever that she was Meg.

*****

Margot woke up the following morning, and saw Bessie sitting by her window. Miles hadn't stayed the night, saying it would be better if he went home and checked on his father. Margot thought there could be

The Return

more to it, but knew he would tell her when he was ready.

'Good morning, Bessie.' She stretched out, raising her arms beyond her pillow, and clasped her hands together. 'What a night. I think it went off quite well, don't you?'

Leaving her chair, Bessie came over to sit on the bed as Margot pulled herself up into a sitting position.

'I's thinking you did very well. But I's also thinking our Lord Brandon has only one option left to stop you marrying Miles, and that's to get rid of you … permanently. I's thinking he's the one we's got to watch out for. Whatever you do from now on, check everything.'

Margot nodded. 'I think you could be right. But, if my vision of Meg's death is true, which I now have no reason to doubt, he will cut through the girth straps, the saddle will come off and Meg with it. The fall will break her neck. That was how she died. I will have to double-check the saddle every time I go riding. Not that I've been riding since I've been here.' Margot frowned, and looked straight at Bessie. 'If I'm still going to be occupying Meg's body, will it be my neck that gets broken?'

'Pon my word, no. Anyway, I's thinking you's already knowing the date of Meg's death from the books you found, and from her headstone. You's been forewarned, and won't gallop off like Meg did. Every time you get on a horse, check that the straps haven't been tampered with first.'

'Hmm, there's one thing neither of us has considered,' she said, thoughtfully. 'What if the date of her death has changed? Could our being here have prompted the murderer to act sooner? Think about it, Meg was never in a position to confront Mr Crankston-Smythe the way we did. Would that be enough to change history?'

Bessie's eyes glazed over. 'I's never knew the name of the murderer. That's not allowed. But I am allowed to find out and stop it if it's not supposed to happen, which is what we're here to do. So, you's might be right. Meg could be murdered any time now.'

They both fell silent, not sure now if they *could* prevent Meg's untimely death.

'I's thinking it's time to let Miles see those documents that incriminate his father and Mr Crankston-Smythe.' Bessie stood up, returning to the window and stared out across the garden. 'I's got a new idea. One that can't fail.'

'That sounds interesting,' Margot said, as she swung her legs out onto the floor. She put her slippers on, and joined her friend. 'Well, tell me, then.'

Bessie grinned. 'I's thinking we'll wait until after Jane has been in to help you dress—'

'Oh crikey. I'd better get ready for her. She'll be

here shortly.'

'You's do that, and leave the papers to me. I hid the parcel so no one could accidentally come across it.' With that, Bessie left the room and Margot started her ablutions.

It wasn't until after Margot had finished her breakfast that she met up with Bessie again. Margot would have suggested a walk, but it was too cold for that. Instead, they went to the library.

'No one will come in; I've left instructions that I'm not to be disturbed. Let's sit down and you can tell me your idea.'

Bessie brought out the neatly wrapped parcel, and placed it on the small tea table in front of them. 'I's thinking it would be too risky to leave it at the mansion. Anyone could get hold of it, and there's no guarantee it would be given to Miles. So, the next time Miles stays the night, I'll put the parcel, addressed for his eyes only, on the front step just before he leaves. He'll know you had nothing to do with it because you would have been with him all the time. And he doesn't know my handwriting. What do you think?'

'I think you're a genius. That solves that problem perfectly. There must be many people who have a grudge to bear against either Lord Brandon or the solicitor. How they got hold of the documents is of no concern to us. We know nothing.' Margot started laughing. 'That will most likely take away the threat of Meg's murder.'

'Hmm, but we's won't be taking any chances. We's have to stay alert. At least until the name of the would-be murderer is discovered, and the known date her murder took place, has passed.'

'You're right, of course.' Margot picked up the package and handed it to Bessie. 'You had better write on it now, and then it will be ready. Oh, I do hope this works. It would be nice to clear Meg's father's name.'

A tap on the door made Margot frown. 'I said I wasn't to be disturbed.' She went over and opened the door. It was Jane. The look on her face told Margot not to be angry. 'What is it, Jane?'

'Sorry to disturb you, Mistress. There's a Lady Crawford wanting to see you.'

The first person Margot thought of was Meg's mother, but she had died. Bessie then reminded her that Meg had a brother. This must be his wife, Gwendolyn.

'Show her into the sitting room, Jane, and tell her I'll be there directly.'

When Jane had gone, Margot looked at Bessie. 'What would she want to see Meg about? And wasn't I told that nobody, including her brother, knew where Meg lived?'

'I's thinking there's a lot we need to find out, and

The Return

there's only one way to do it. I's be coming, too.'

When Margot walked into the sitting room, she was surprised to see her visitor dressed head to toe in black, with a black net veil over her face.

'Lady Gwendolyn? This is an unexpected surprise. Please, sit, I'll call for refreshments.'

'There will be no need for that, thank you, Lady Margaret. I've come here myself because I believe it's the decent thing to do. I'm sorry to have to inform you, but your brother died suddenly. Obviously, because you were estranged, you weren't mentioned in his will.' She looked around the room. 'But it seems you've been *kept* quite comfortable here. I won't delay you any longer. You will receive a message regarding the funeral in due time.' With that, she turned on her heel and walked out the room.

Margot stared at the closed door. 'What a bitch.'

Sandra Stoner-Mitchell

25

'And to think I actually felt sorry for her.'
Margot fumed at the woman's bad
manners. 'And how would she know
what's in Richard's will? If he hasn't been buried,
then surely it wouldn't have been read yet? And won't
it have to go to probate first? From what I learned
about Meg's brother, I doubt he would have sat down
and discussed any of this with Gwendolyn.'

'I's thinking you could be right. Not that I's
understanding a lot about such things.' Bessie went
over to sit on the couch. 'You's could always ask
Miles. He'd be knowing.'

'Yes, I will … And did you hear the way she said
I've been *kept* comfortable? *Kept*. How dare she
insinuate Meg is a kept woman. I wish now I'd been

The Return

quicker and slapped that superior look off her supercilious face before she left.'

Margot was pacing up and down the sitting room; skirts swishing, hands on hips, and her green eyes blazing. Bessie thought she looked ready to chase after Meg's sister-in-law and give her something more painful than a piece of her mind.

Bessie couldn't help smiling at Margot acting so indignant. She realised it was only because the lady, whose body she was sharing, had been insulted in such a vulgar way.

'I's thinking you should forget that spiteful woman for now, Margot, and calm down. We's got other things to think about, more urgent than Meg's reputation.   That will never be a problem, especially after last night.'

Margot stopped pacing and flopped down on the couch next to Bessie. 'Do you want another cup of tea? I do. I'd have something stronger if it was later in the day.' She stood up again and went to pull the bell-cord that rang in the kitchen.

Moments later, the door opened. 'Ah, Jane, would you take a pot of tea to the library room for me, please?'

The maid bobbed a curtsy, and smiled. 'Right away, Mistress.'

Margot waited until the door had been closed before speaking to Bessie. 'Come on, it's better in the library. We'll not be overheard in there.

After Jane had delivered the pot of tea, and they were alone again, Margot brought out Bessie's hidden cup from the little drawer under the table and poured their tea.

'I's thinking that when Miles comes in, I's'll go and see what Gwendolyn's up to. There were something about her behaviour that rankled. I's thinking to meself her husband's death were a bit sudden. It's not as if he were old, he weren't much older than his sister.'

'Really?' Margot took a sip of her hot brew, then took out a notepad and pencil from the same drawer she'd kept Bessie's cup. 'I just thought she was being her usual nasty self. But if you think there's more to it, then it's worth checking out.'

'It's just a feeling. But when I's getting them, I's knowing something is up.'

'Okay. Miles didn't say what time he's coming, so let's go over what we've discovered so far, and what we still need to find. Who it could be, why he, *or* she, wants Meg dead; and most importantly, how we can prove it and prevent it from happening. At the moment, the last two need a lot more thought.'

Margot picked up the pencil and, after she'd touched the tip of the sharpened graphite with her tongue, she wrote down Lord Brandon's name. 'I think it's him; no one else comes close to being capable of murder.'

'I's thinking he'll be in the top three.'

'Top three. Crikey, Bessie, how many people do you think want to kill Meg?' Margot was gobsmacked.

'Lord Brandon, Mr Crankston-Smythe, Lady Gwendolyn, and I's thinking there's one more. But I's got some snooping to do before I's giving you the name.'

Margot racked her brain for another person to be a consideration, but ended up shaking her head, completely baffled.

'Okay, I'll put down the three obvious names. Now we know Gwendolyn knew where Meg lived, I suppose it's safe to say the other's do, as well. Although I still can't see how any of them can get close enough to interfere with Meg's saddle without someone seeing them.'

She added both names, then tapped her lips with the end of the pencil as she thought what to add next.

'We've got to consider what reason any of them would have. One thing is certain, Lord Brandon most definitely doesn't want his son to marry Meg. I think his reasons are rather iffy, especially as we haven't a clue what motivated him to cheat Meg's father out of his entire estate. Why would he deliberately go out of his way to do such a thing? Certainly not for money. As far as we can determine, he's got enough of his own. I think there's more to this than meets the eye, and we need to find out what it is as soon as possible.'

Bessie flinched; her eyes glazed over and her facial expression became quite unreadable. It was at times like this that Margot wished she could mind-read. While her friend was mulling it over in her head, she could only sit, be quiet, and wait.

To fill in time, Margot wrote down the reason the solicitor might have to want Meg dead. In fact, that was quite easy. He knew she was on to him. Getting rid of Meg would rid him of the threat of being disbarred, and worse, sent to prison.

But Lady Gwendolyn? There is no valid reason why she would want Meg dead. Yes, she hated her sister-in-law, but what would she gain by murdering her … unless she's worried Meg might be mentioned in Richard's will. I suppose she would be upset to see all her personal things shared amongst the people she hated.

Without any warning, Bessie sprung up from her chair and spun around to face Margot. 'When you said there was more to this than we know, you were right. But for some strange reason, I's not recalling what it is. There is more … I's thinking some discreet probing into Lord Brandon's past is what needs to be done to help me remember. I's wondering if there is another story behind all this.'

Bessie started pacing the room, hands clasped

behind her, and every so often she'd nod her head.

'Yes, I's going to be busy for the next few hours. I's thinking Lady Gwendolyn's impertinent butler has a part to play in this as well.'

'You're certainly coming up with the suspects. How are you going to sort through them all?'

'I's got my ways,' Bessie said, but didn't elaborate. 'Is Miles staying tonight? I's asking because I's gonna be busy for a few hours and want to be back to put the package on the step before he leaves.'

'I'll make sure he stays, at least until I you're back and you've done the deed.' Margot chuckled. 'This is really exciting, and a bit cloak and daggerish.'

Bessie had to laugh. 'What else have you's put down on your notepad?'

'Not a lot. I was trying to work out what reason the other two had to harm Meg, and realised they all had motives. It's just working out which of them is the would-be-murderer.'

'I's thinking there's not much we can do now until we've got the rest of the evidence, so I's off to pay Gwendolyn a visit now.'

'You do that, and I'll carry on searching here. Not sure what for, but it will give me something to do.'

*****

Miles stood in front of his father and watched him

for a moment. He was sitting at his desk, leaning on his elbows with his head dropped into his hands.

'You don't look very well, Father. A hangover, perhaps? Not that I've any sympathy for you. You deserve all you get after that disgraceful display you put on last night.'

Lord Brandon lifted his head, winced, and glared at his son. 'None of this would have happened had you not gone ahead and disobeyed me. Goodness knows how this will affect your mother's health, or if she will survive it.'

'Don't you think you and Mother have overplayed this … this charade? It's balderdash and you know it.' Miles almost spat the words out. He was finding it hard to keep his temper under control. 'It just so happens I've recently discovered Mother is as fit as we are. Why you have both lied all these years, is beyond me.'

Now it was Lord Brandon's turn to flare up in anger. The blood drained from his face as he lurched forward, flattening his hands on the desk, and pushed himself up. 'How dare you call your mother and me liars, Sir. You have gone too far. Get out of my sight.'

As if the strain was too great, he fell back on his chair, clutching his chest.

'Ah, so it's a heart attack now, is it?' Miles sneered. 'I'm sorry, Father, I'm not playing this game anymore. I'm going back to see Meg and apologise for your rudeness. Oh, but before I go, will you tell Mother how pleased I was to see her last week in the park? It seems a miracle has occurred. To see her out and about, laughing with friends, was surprising enough, but to see her riding the *stallion*, *and* controlling him the way she did, was extraordinary for a woman, but an absolute miracle for a frail invalid. Perhaps you both thought I was away?' With that, Miles spun on his heel and marched out the room, deliberately slamming the door.

*****

Margot had searched every inch of the attic, so didn't bother to go up there again. She stood in the library, staring at the hundreds of books on display.

It will take me forever to open them all in the unlikely event of finding another letter.

'Okay. If I wanted to hide a note in a book, which would be the best one to put it in?' Her eyes scanned across the many rows of books, but none jumped out at her. She let her eyes travel up.

'One that is out of reach and one that is the least likely to be taken down.'

Margot was looking around for something to stand on when she heard a scream and then a crash. 'What the hell was that?'

She rushed from the room, and seeing Jane dash into the sitting room, she followed. When she went through the doorway, she stopped. Jane was helping a maid who had cut her head.

Margot's first priority was for the girl. 'Get some water and a cloth, Jane, and something to wrap around the cut.' When Jane rushed out, Margot made the girl sit down, and taking a handkerchief from her pocket, she gently dabbed at the blood trickling down her forehead, so she could see the wound.

'It's not as bad as it looks, dear. How do you feel?'

The girl burst out crying. 'I'm sorry, Mistress, I didn't mean to do it,' she said, with tears pouring down her face.

'Of course you didn't, dear. It was an accident.' It was then Margot saw the picture smashed on the floor. The picture was of no consequence, but what was sticking out the back, was…

The Return

26

When Jane returned with the water and bandage, Margot finished cleaning the wound and wrapped the bandage around the young girl's head.

'That should be fine, Mary. I'll take another look at it in a couple of days. Keep the bandage dry, and if you feel unwell, let Jane know and she will come and tell me.' Margot smiled at the girl, trying to show her she wasn't in trouble. 'Do you feel up to telling me what happened?'

Mary sniffed and wiped her nose on her sleeve. She looked up at Margot, who saw immediately how terrified the young girl was, and hastened to reassure her.

'You are not in trouble, Mary. I need to know these things so that I can ensure it doesn't occur again.'

Mary nodded and looked down at the floor. 'I was standin' on the chair so I could reach t' dust the top of the picture, an' … an' I still couldn't reach it. I tried t' stand on me tippy-toes an' when I reached up … when I reached up, the chair moved away an' I slipped, an' … an' I grabs the picture an' … an' it came down wiv me, too.' Mary turned red-rimmed, beseeching eyes towards Margot, and hiccupped and sniffed as she tried to get the words out. 'I'm sorry, Mistress.'

'Oh Mary, you could have broken an arm or a leg. Why didn't you get the steps to stand on? They would have been a lot safer than a chair.' Margot turned to Jane, who was about to pick up the picture.

'Leave that for the time being, Jane. I want you to take Mary to the kitchen and ask Cook to make her a cup of tea with plenty of sugar. That'll help to calm her down.'

Left alone, Margot allowed herself to focus completely on the taunting, yellowed envelope that had revealed itself when the picture frame had been broken. Taking a deep breath, she pushed herself up from the sofa and, never once taking her eyes off her target, went over and dropped to her knees.

Margot stared at it for the shortest of moments, then, with slow, gentle movements, she carefully eased the fragile envelope from its hidden sanctuary.

Back on the sofa, she opened the letter and began

The Return

reading. Margot's hands trembled; her heart thumped with disturbing rapidity as she realised what she was holding. *Oh Miles, you aren't going to like this.*

Someone chose that moment to tap on the door. Startled, Margot quickly folded the letter and put it back into the envelope. Not bothering to call out, she went and opened the door herself. It was Jane.

'Shall I sort out the picture now, Mistress? I'll see if the frame can be repaired.'

'That's a good idea, Jane. Yes, do that. I have to go up to my room for a while. Should anyone need me, you'll know where I am.'

Margot's thoughts were jumbled with excitement, but also with sadness. Her dilemma was, should she show it to Miles? *This is going to hurt him and yet, he does need to know.*

Deciding to discuss it with Bessie, she unfolded the letter and read it again.

Dearest Emma, or should I now address you formally and call you Lady Emma Caruthers?

My heart breaks knowing you will never stand by my side as my beloved wife. How can it be that your father has given your hand in marriage to William Crawford, knowing I was about to ask for your hand myself?

It was either a show of very bad manners, or there was another reason why he chose to ignore the note I sent asking to speak to him. Of course he knew it was to ask his permission to court you. What hurts—no— what angers me most is the way it was done. It led me to wonder if the Brandon name was not good enough. Did your father have higher aspirations? That thought was dismissed immediately. He has, in fact, married you off to a family far beneath your station, your father being a Baron, and second cousin to Queen Victoria.

There is only one way this could have happened—you asked your father to favour Lord Crawford's proposal over mine. This then led me to believe that you have been seeing that man behind my back. I can think of no other reason your father would do this. You leave me a broken, disappointed and, might I also add, a very angry man.

Charles.

Margot put the letter down. 'Could this be the motive we've been looking for? Lord Brandon never forgave Meg's mother for marrying Lord Crawford. But after all this time, surely, he wouldn't be that petty. He found love again with Lady Brandon … didn't he? Why would he begrudge his son his happiness? And why ruin Lord Crawford?'

*****

The Return

Bessie had entered Lady Gwendolyn's home, arriving at the most opportune moment. The lady was enjoying a cup of tea with her butler—who was holding her hand.

Well, well, well. This is a surprise. Bessie's eyebrows nearly shot up past her hairline. *I's wondering what their story is.*

'You must have faith that Richard disliked his sister more than he disliked you, my dear. But if you are still worried….'

Gwendolyn's head snapped up and stared into Jenkins' eyes. 'If I could be certain that Margaret isn't in the will, I would be fine. But this has been my family's home for three hundred years.
I won't see it split up and shared with Richard's sister. Why should I?'

'Margaret is the last surviving member of the Crawford family. If she should accidentally die, that would solve everything.'

Gwendolyn smiled. 'You are the only good person in my life, Jenkins, always have been. I just hope my son doesn't turn out to be like his father and grandfather.' A little smile hovered over her face, surprising Bessie at how pretty it made Gwendolyn look. Motherhood suited her.

'But it won't be easy to poison her the way we did my father and Richard,' she continued. The warm moment disappeared as her slumped shoulders revealed her sense of hopelessness.

'Why don't you leave that to me, my dear? We've come this far; you can't give up now. Soon you won't be answerable to anyone. I promise you.' He lifted her hand and, bringing it to his lips, gently kissed it.

Gwendolyn reached out and stroked the side of his face. 'I would never have got through my childhood, let alone the latter years, without you in my life, Jenkins. I'm so pleased you were father's butler. You've been more of a father to me than he ever was, and I've loved you as such. But how I wish things were different.'

'There are good men out there, my dear. If I were forty years younger … well, who knows what might have been? Come, let's do something to cheer you up.'

Bessie had heard enough. She needed to get out of the house before she started feeling sorry for Gwendolyn, which she knew she would under different circumstances.

So here we have a new suspect, and from what Jenkins said, he could get rid of Meg in a different way. Perhaps he is the one who will mess with the saddle.

*****

Lord Brandon's home was a hive of activity when Bessie made her way inside. The kitchen staff were

The Return

busy preparing the evening meal, and from what Bessie could see, it wasn't just for two people. *Was Miles joining his parents this evening?*

Bessie wandered around the rooms, and couldn't find Lord Brandon anywhere. She made her way upstairs. Walking past the bedrooms which led off the corridor, she was surprised to hear some angry voices coming from the room that had its door slightly opened. Curious, Bessie managed to open it enough to squeeze inside.

'You are useless. If you can't stop your son from doing as he pleases, I shall have to do it myself. I'll make sure the marriage doesn't take place … ever. That whore's daughter is not going to live here and call herself Lady Brandon. Do you understand me?'

'How do you think you're going to stop it? Commit bloody murder? Don't be such a fool, woman. I've put up with your selfishness and stupidity long enough. Why don't you grow up.'

Bessie thought Lord Brandon was about to leave, but his wife spoke again. Her cold, sinister voice carried an ominous threat.

'You want to be careful how you speak to me, Charles. Don't forget, I know what you did to Lord Crawford. Just one word in the right ear and all your cronies will hear about it.'

'Really? Just listen to yourself. Do you think I don't know what you've been up to all these years?

Sandra Stoner-Mitchell

You say one word to my *cronies*, just one single word, and you'll see what real revenge is like. How many women will want to invite you to their coffee mornings, or afternoon teas when they find out you've been bedding their husbands? You'll not be able to show your face in public again.'

This time, when Lord Brandon made to leave, a silver-backed hand mirror was thrown towards the back of his head. But missing, it shattered on the door.

I's thinking Margot and I's got our work cut out discovering which of these people wants to kill Meg. She's the only innocent one amongst the lot of them.

Bessie was just about to leave when she heard a knock at the door. She went down the stairs, curious as to who the visitor might be.'

The butler had opened the door, and, surprise, surprise, there stood Mr Crankston-Smythe.

'His Lordship is expecting you, Sir. If you'll follow me.'

Well now, this will be interesting. I's thinking I's going to invite myself to the party.

The Return

27

When Lord Brandon marched into the reception room, his foul mood was instantly apparent. The atmosphere cooled to somewhere below freezing. Roger Crankston-Smythe was already regretting his decision to come.

Expecting a long wait, the solicitor had just made himself comfortable on the sofa. He leapt to his feet and held out his hand, withdrawing it moments later when he realised it was being snubbed, as Brandon spoke, deliberately mis-pronouncing his name, 'It's a bit late in the day for a visit, Smith. What's so important that it couldn't wait until morning? I don't have much time to spare, so make it quick.'

Ignorant bastard. The solicitor ignored Lord Brandon deliberately miss pronouncing his name.

'I thought you might like to know that we have a problem regarding Lord Crawford. He's not at all happy with what we've done to his wife and daughter.' The words came out in a rush, and no sooner had he said it, he wished he hadn't. This wasn't going as planned.

Lord Brandon stared at him as if he was seeing his solicitor for the first time. Then his stunned silence gave way to a cold, humourless laugh. 'Okay, joke's over. I don't have time for this. What do you want? Come on, man, out with it. You're sorely testing my temper.'

'It's no joke, Lord Brandon, I did receive a visit from Mistress Crawford, and the ghost of her father. You can believe it or not. I really don't care anymore. That lady knows what we did.'

There was an immediate change in Lord Brandon's features. His eyes bulged, and his flabby, blotched cheeks turned purple. 'Are you out of your tiny mind?' his voice boomed out, scaring the life out of the solicitor. 'Have you been drinking, sir?'

It might have taken every ounce of courage he possessed, but Roger didn't so much as flinch. 'No, I'm neither drunk nor mad, sir.' He stood straight, with shoulders back, and his chin thrust out. 'I'm telling you that I had a visit from Mistress Crawford and her father … and before you say it, I know he's dead. I wouldn't have believed it myself had he not started throwing things around the room. Now, if you'll just take a moment to listen, I'll tell you what Mistress Margaret told me. They know what we did and she's threatening to tell everyone.'

Bessie was glad they couldn't see her. She'd never before had the satisfaction of seeing, and enjoying, a scene instigated by something she'd done. This was hilarious. She couldn't wait to tell Margot.

Lord Brandon shook his head. 'You're an absolute idiot. You want to be careful who you talk to. If this gets out, you'll be laughed out of society. There are no such things as ghosts. What exactly did that damned woman tell you?'

'She said she had written proof of what we've done, and wants her father's good name restored.'

'Well, there you have it. The woman is an obvious liar. Did you ask her to show you the written proof? No, I thought not,' he said, before the solicitor could answer. 'She would have had to get into my office to gain that. And I can tell you now, that woman hasn't been anywhere near my home since I forbade Miles to marry her.'

The first inklings of doubt flitted across Roger's face. Had he imagined it? Was it all a trick? He frowned, then looked Charles Brandon in the eye.

'We'll leave it like that then, shall we? I've told you what I know, so now we'll have to wait and see if the lady talks to anyone else.' Not wanting to stay in Lord Brandon's presence a moment longer than necessary, he picked up his hat, and nodded. 'Good day to you, Sir.'

After he'd gone, Bessie stared at the man scowling at the door. Then, looking around the room, a little smile crept over her face. She picked up the poker standing by the open fire, and marching up to Lord Brandon, she tapped him on the shoulder with it.

'What the hell...' He spun around and saw nothing but a poker—levitating on its own, right in front of his eyes. His body twitched convulsively as he tried to move his feet that were determined not to obey.

'What sorcery is this? Show yourself.... You ... don't scare me ... I know it's you, Crawford ... get away from me—'

When Bessie held the poker high, his confused, terrified eyes followed its rise; she held it there a moment longer, teasing, giving it a little wiggle before letting it drop. The resulting clunk as it hit the floor was enough to release Lord Brandon's feet and give him the courage to turn and run from the room.

Bessie laughed, and, delighted with the result, followed him out, and left.

*****

Before entering the house, Bessie satisfied herself that Miles' horse wasn't in the stable. Bessie was pleased as it meant she would be able to catch Margot before he arrived. She had much to tell her.

'Bessie. Close the door, I don't want anyone to come in. Oh, I'm so glad you're back. I have a dilemma, and I need your advice.'

'I's thinking we's both got a lot to share.' Bessie walked over and sat beside Margot. 'You's go first.'

Margot described what had happened, how she'd seen the letter poking out the back of the broken picture frame. Then, sitting back, she passed it over for Bessie to read.

'Now that explains a lot.' Bessie paused for a moment before saying, 'I's just been listening to an interesting conversation.' She went on to tell Margot all she'd learned.

'Lady Crawford rejected him? So, what this letter says is all true and Lady Brandon must have known of it. It all makes sense now. No wonder they don't want Miles to marry Meg. What do we do now?'

'I's thinking we's carry on as we'd planned. I's going to leave the package on the doorstep before Miles leaves. It's time he knew what's been going on.'

'I agree. But what about this letter?' Margot took it from Bessie and put it back in the envelope. 'Shall I show Miles?'

Bessie's face twisted into a comical frown, lips pursed, eyes staring up to her eyebrows, then she nodded. 'Yes, I's thinking that'll be good. You's can tell him you think you knows why his dad doesn't like you. Explain what happened with the picture and then let him read it.'

'Okay. I'll do that. Did you go to Gwendolyn's house?

'Oh yes. It won't upset you, but I's not sure about Meg, though. Gwendolyn and Jenkins, her butler, done Richard and her father in. Killed them both, they did. And, she don't really know if you've been left anything in the will or not. So they's thinking you's going to be killed next.'

'I see. Well, that's interesting. They are Meg's murderers.'

'Well, not necessarily. I's also got my eyes on Lady Brandon. She will do anything to stop Miles marrying Meg. And she's not the feeble lady that Miles was brought up to believe.'

Bessie and Margot lapsed into silence, both thinking about what they'd learned.

'What happens now with Gwendolyn and her butler? They have already murdered two people. I don't know what Meg will think. I mean, they weren't close by a long shot. But he was still her brother, and to be murdered, well…' Margot sucked on her bottom lip as she thought of her next question. 'Will they be found out?'

'I's thinking theys won't. Not unless there's some suspicion. His last words mentioned murder, but no

The Return

names. And only the people in the gentlemen's club were there. I's thinking many of those men wouldn't lift a finger to help, but a few might have wanted him dead. Who's to know?'

Hearing the door, Margot gave Bessie a warning look. Miles had arrived. Bessie pointed to the letter.

When Miles burst into the room, Margot could tell at a glance something was wrong. She sprang to her feet. 'Miles? What's the matter?'

Seeing Margot's worried look, Miles chided himself immediately going over and taking her into his arms. 'Nothing for you to be worried about, my sweet Meg. Not now that I have you crushed against my heart.'

His soft, warm voice reassured Margot and she relaxed again. 'You looked so angry when you came in, I couldn't help feeling concerned.'

'Anyone would be in a foul mood after listening to my father. I will never understand that man. All I can hope for is that I don't end up like him.'

'You are nothing like him, and never could be.' She took a deep breath and gently pulled away. 'I think I know why your father doesn't want you to marry me, Miles.'

He frowned. 'Oh, apart from the reason that he is totally out of his tiny mind? Come, let's sit down and you can tell me your thoughts.' He gave her one of his dazzling smiles and kissed the tip of her nose.

'Wait a minute, I have something to show you.' Margot fetched the letter and came to sit with him. She explained what had happened, and what she found tucked in the back of the painting.

'This is it. I wasn't sure whether to show you or not, but … well, here it is.' She passed it over, glancing across at Bessie, who was still in the room. Miles took the letter out of the envelope and sat back to read it. Margot watched his face for any reaction, but apart from a slight lift of his eyebrows and a twitch in his cheek, he showed no other response.

Finally, Margot couldn't wait any longer. 'Miles? What are you thinking? Will this make a difference to us?'

'What? Oh no. Not the slightest. If anything, this letter has answered so many questions that have plagued me for years. I couldn't understand why Father was so adamant about us not getting married. Now, at least I can see what he has been harbouring all these years. It also makes me wonder if the contents of this letter are the underlying reason my mother has behaved the way she has. It still doesn't excuse them, though.' He folded the letter and put it back in the envelope. 'Would you mind if I borrowed this? I'm going back to have it out with Father.'

Bessie vigorously shook her head. 'I's not got the package yet. You's got to keep him here.'

Margot tilted her head and gave Miles a coy smile.

The Return

'You don't have to go straight away … do you? I was hoping—'

Miles grinned, stood and pulled her up. 'There is no reason whatsoever for me to go yet.' Without another word, he picked Margot up, and walked towards the door.

'I's thinking it's not all acting.' Bessie chuckled as Margot was whisked out of the room.

28

Bessie stood back to observe Miles as he stepped outside, and held her breath when she saw him stand on the large parcel wrapped in brown paper she'd placed right in front of the door. When he picked it up, Bessie watched as he read the addressee's name.

Now he knows it's for him.

He turned the package over, giving it a cursory glance before looking around. Apart from herself, whom Miles couldn't see, there was no one else in sight. He then appeared to come to a decision; he took it with him and put it in his saddlebag.

'I's thinking you's gonna be a mite angry soon, young man.' With a satisfied smile, Bessie went inside to let Margot know their plan had worked.

The Return

*****

Sarah Fellowes tapped on the door of her husband's home office, and entered, carrying a tray of coffee with a plate of fresh baked coconut biscuits. 'I thought you two might be in need of some light refreshment.'

Miles leaned back on his chair and raked his hand through his hair, pushing an annoying lock off his face. 'You must have read my mind, Sarah. I need something to wash out the nasty taste in my mouth.'

At the tone of his voice, Joshua looked across at Miles and saw the anger blazing in his eyes. 'You've every right to be cross, Miles. From what these letters reveal, your father, with the help of Mr Crankston-Smythe, deliberately set out to destroy Lord Crawford. We already know they succeeded. What I don't know is, and I doubt you do either, what did they do with Lord Crawford's estate after it was sold? He didn't lose it gambling, as everyone was led to believe, so who has the money?'

Sarah put the tray down on the desk and poured three coffees. 'Does Meg know about any of this?'

At the mention of Meg's name, Miles groaned. His head dropped back, as if to study the ceiling, then scrunched his eyes closed. 'Meg. Oh, my dear, sweet Meg, what has my family done to you?'

Taking a deep breath, he pulled himself together and sat up. 'No, she knows none of this. And now I have to tell her. I could hardly blame her if she wants nothing more to do with me.'

Joshua leapt in to support his lifelong friend. 'This is not your fault, Miles. What your father has done is despicable, but Meg already knows the reason why. I can't imagine him carrying a torch for Meg's mother for all those years. I didn't think he was capable of such an emotion. But, unrequited love and all that...'

'Yes, that was a shock.' Miles looked down at the letter in front of him. 'I'm going to pay Mr Crankston-Smythe a visit. I want to get some answers from him before I confront my father. Thanks, Sarah.' He took the cup of coffee from her hand and took a sip.

Joshua looked doubtful. 'Don't be surprised if he doesn't answer your questions. He'll know his career and his freedom could be in jeopardy if he owns up to any of this.'

'As if I give a damn—Forgive me, Sarah, I didn't mean to swear in front of you.' *Get a grip, man.* 'This has got me so incensed. If he knows what's good for him, he *will* answer my questions. I know Crankston-Smythe wouldn't have instigated this. And even if he *had* come up with the idea, he certainly wouldn't have approached my father. No, he just did as he was told.'

'Mmm, I have to agree with you. Is there anything I can do?'

Miles raised his hands. 'No, I've got to do this. Thanks, Josh.' He turned to Sarah. 'You've both done more than enough to help, and I really appreciate it.'

*****

Margot had come to a decision. She'd mulled it over since Bessie had told her about Gwendolyn and her butler.

'I'm going to pay Gwendolyn a visit,' she said, startling Bessie who was doodling on a piece of paper. 'And you're coming with me.'

'And just what are you's hoping to achieve?'

'For a start, it will take one would-be-murderer out of the picture. When I tell her I know what she and her butler have been up to, and what their next plan is, well … well, we'll see what happens.'

'I's thinking it might work. But shouldn't you's go to the police and report them? Then they would both be out of it.'

'I did think of that, but what proof do I have? I can't go to the police and say, "hi there, my invisible friend overheard Lady Crawford and her butler talking about how they'd murdered her father *and* her husband," can I? I'd most likely end up having Meg put into a mental institution.'

Bessie chuckled. 'Put like that, no, I's not thinking yous can. Okay, when do yous want to do this?'

'No time like the present. You can be my backup … do what you did in Crankston-Smythe's office. You enjoyed that, didn't you?'

'It was fun. I's thinking Gwendolyn just might be scared enough to change her mind about doing you in.'

Margot grinned, remembering the look on the solicitor's face. 'Come on, I'll call for the carriage, then grab my coat.'

'I's thinking it would be a good idea if'n you's bring a piece of paper and a pencil with you.'

'Oh?' Margot squinted, as she gave Bessie a puzzled look.

'I's thinking that a letter from her late departed father might just spook her enough not to do anything stupid ... like murder Meg.'

Margot's eyes sparkled as a smile spread over her face. 'What are you thinking of writing? We need to word it as if it is the ghost of her father.'

'You's right about that. Let's see. If'n you were Gwendolyn's father, what would you's say?'

'I'd say, "You spoilt brat. After all I did for you. Found you a nice lord to marry so you could be a lady. And then you had the audacity to poison me—me, your own father. And your dear husband? He's not very happy with you, either. If you kill his sister, he won't like that. So be warned. If you do, we'll be waiting for you when you die, watch out." What do you think?'

Bessie laughed. 'You's wanting me to write that? I's thinking it'd be grand, but I's gonna have a bit of trouble remembering all that.'

Margot thought for a moment, her index finger tapping her lips. 'Hmn. Let's cut it down a bit. What about we keep the bit about her being a spoilt brat? Then we can add a bit that will scare the life out of her.'

'I's thinking I's gonna need to practice that. Give me the pencil.'

After a few tries, and lots of laughter, Bessie and Margot finally agreed on what Bessie should write.

Fifteen minutes later, Margot and Bessie were on their way to see Lady Crawford. Margot's stomach was full of butterflies as she thought about how her conversation would go. The fact that she knew Gwendolyn was capable of murder didn't ease her state of mind.

The butler answered the door after Margot had given the cast-iron door knocker a resounding bang.

'I'm here to see Lady Crawford,' Margot said, bringing out her most commanding voice. 'Please inform her ladyship that Lady Margaret Crawford is here to see her.'

'Lady Crawford is not receiving visitors. It would have been advisable to have sent a message before you came. You would have been saved this fruitless journey.'

'I's thinking this snotty butler needs taking down a peg or two.'

Sandra Stoner-Mitchell

Margot gave the man standing in front of her a steely look. 'Hmm, is that so? Then perhaps you should inform Lady Crawford that if she doesn't see me now, this minute, the police will be her next visitors. That also includes a visit to you, as well, Jenkins.' Margot had the satisfaction of seeing him flinch but he was quick to recover.

'If you would like to wait, I will find out.' With that, he shut the door in Margot's face.

Bessie's fury knew no bounds as she glared at the closed door. 'I's thinking I'm going to enjoy bringing you down.'

A smile flitted across Margot's face as she anticipated her friend's vengeance. Before she could ask Bessie what else she planned, the door flew open and the butler stood aside to allow them to pass.

'Her ladyship will make an exception; only because you are her sister-in-law.'

Margot breezed past him and simply nodded. Jenkins closed the door and walked ahead. 'If you would follow me.'

When Jenkins ushered them into the sitting room, Gwendolyn was sitting on the sofa facing the door. Her stiff back, and white knuckles resting on her lap, were the first things Margot noticed. When Gwendolyn looked up, Margot was sure she saw a flash of nervousness in her eyes, but it was replaced so quickly by a hard, frigid coldness, she had to wonder if she'd imagined it.

'Good morning, Gwendolyn. I'm sorry for calling on you so early in the day, but it was necessary.'

Hearing the door close behind her, Margot turned. Jenkins had stayed in the room. 'I'm glad you saw fit to remain, since this concerns you as well.'

'I wish you would get on and say what you came to say, instead of talking in riddles, Margaret. Just say what you have to say, then go.' Gwendolyn stood up and went to stand beside Jenkins. 'I take it Miles knows you're here?'

'What has Miles got to do with this? I'm here of my own volition, Gwendolyn.'

'Jenkins said you mentioned going to the police. I think that rather foolish of someone who appears to be intelligent. Supposing we decide to keep you here, in the cellar? Who would know?' She moved closer to Jenkins, who put a protective arm around her.

Margot grinned and moved over to sit on the sofa. 'I'm not alone, Gwendolyn. Now, it seems you've managed to get away with poisoning your father and my brother. Fine, Richard and I were never close, so…' She shrugged dismissively. 'But you can think again about murdering me. I'm sorry to have to ruin your plans. It's not going to happen.'

'You seem to be very sure of yourself.' Jenkins said, as he pointedly looked around the room. 'So, where is the other person? You said you weren't alone.'

'That's right.' Margot gave Gwendolyn a frosty glare. 'There is someone here who is not at all happy with you, my dear. In fact, he's more than a little annoyed. He mentioned something about you discovering a plant called hemlock in the garden?'

29

For a moment, no-one said a word. With increasing amusement, Margot watched the muscles working in the faces of both Gwendolyn and Jenkins. Then Gwendolyn's harsh, embittered voice cut into the silence.

'When we were first married, Margaret, your dear departed brother told me that your imagination bordered on the psychotic. I thought at the time he was just being true to his contemptuous nature. But, my word, I can now see he was right. But let's pretend for a moment that what you've just said *is* true, even though it's not, what makes you think we won't get away with it? I see no one coming to stop us.'

This was going a hundred times better than Margot ever thought it would. She smiled and turned to Bessie. 'What do you think, Mr Turnbull?'

Gwendolyn threw Jenkins a quick glance before returning her attention to Margot. She smirked.

'You've just said that I murdered my father, and now you're telling us he's in the room? You *are* insane.'

'Of course, you can't see him, can you? What was I thinking?' Margot chuckled. 'Now, this is what I understand is going on so far. I've already mentioned that I know you murdered your father and husband … with a little bit of help from Romeo there,' she said, nodding towards Jenkins. 'And I *know* you're both making plans to murder me. And why do you need to murder me? Let's see now. Even though you told me on your visit that I wasn't mentioned in Richard's will, you can't really be sure, can you? And for that reason alone, just in case I am, you want me out of the way. Well, let me reassure you. I can actually tell you, Gwendolyn, without even seeing the will, Richard most assuredly would not have mentioned me. The main reason being, he probably despised me more than he detested you.'

Jenkins took a step closer to Margot. 'You think you know it all, don't you? But you don't. Lady Crawford is a respected and well-liked member of society so I insist you stop upsetting her with all your lies and outlandish ideas. If not, it will be me calling the police. Everything you've said is unsubstantiated. You can't prove a thing.'

The Return

'Oh, but I can, Jenkins.' She turned to Bessie, grinning mischievously. 'Mr Turnbull? The floor is yours.' Margot sat back on the sofa and crossed her legs, her eyes fixed on Gwendolyn.

This was what Bessie had been waiting for, and she was going to relish every moment. She walked up to Gwendolyn, pushed the loose ringlet off her face, and then gave her cheek a light tweak.

'Ouch.' Simultaneously startled and spooked, Gwendolyn stepped back. Her hands flew to her face. 'What was that?'

'What was what?' Jenkins looked at her, his frown pulling his dark, wiry brows together, reminding Margot of the bristle brush her mother used to clean the oven racks with.

'Something pinched me.'

'There's nothing here. It's her— she's putting suggestions into your head.' Jenkins grabbed Gwendolyn's shoulders and pulled her into his arms, one hand stroking her hair, soothing her. 'I think you'd better go, now.' he told Margot. 'We don't tolerate witchcraft in this country. It's fortunate for you we no longer burn witches at the stake.'

Bessie chuckled, and even Margot had to laugh.

'Witchcraft, is it? I's gonna show them what witchcraft looks like.' With an idea already forming after she'd seen the fire glowing in the grate, and the tray of drinks on the highly polished walnut sideboard, she dashed over and picked up the decanter of whisky and a glass. She smiled. 'I's thinking that'll do nicely.'

Gwendolyn and Jenkins were rooted to the spot, their eyes widening, as they watched the decanter and glass moving through the air. When the items stopped in front of the fireplace, Jenkins appeared to come out of his stupor. He took Gwendolyn's hand in his and turned to leave the room.

'You don't scare me at all. Come, Gwendolyn, we'll leave and get the men to escort her out.'

Margot got to the door first, and stood in front, barring the way. 'Not so fast, you two. Mr Turnbull has not finished yet. Don't you know it's the height of rudeness to leave the show when it's still playing? You wouldn't want to upset your father any more, Gwendolyn, would you?'

The speed at which Gwendolyn shook her head had Margot worried that she'd do herself a mischief.

Bessie had taken the top off the decanter and poured some of the whisky into the glass. Making sure she had her audience's attention; she threw it onto the hot coals. The embers flared into high, angry swirls of red and blue flames, roaring up the chimney. The sight was incredible. Bessie laughed. She was beginning to enjoy playing a ghost.

Once the alcohol had been consumed by the flames, the fire resumed its lazy smouldering. Although tempted to do it again, Bessie didn't want to risk setting the place on fire. Seeing Gwendolyn's and Jenkins' dropped jaws, and the terror in their eyes, she smiled. She had produced the effect she was looking for.

Before her finále, she decided to teach Jenkins a lesson. She marched up to him, and with her thumb beneath his dropped jaw, she pushed it up, closing his mouth. He shook his head, waving his hands trying to ward off the evil ghost. But Bessie had already moved on.

'Let me have that piece of paper, and the pencil, Margot.' Bessie waited while Margot took them from her handbag, all the while watched by Meg's sister-in-law and Jenkins. They stared with growing fear and consternation as the paper and pencil moved, seemingly of their own accord, over to the table. The room was silent as the pencil appeared to write on the paper.

When it floated over to Gwendolyn, she was far too scared to touch it. Bessie held it up so both of them could read it.

You spoilt brat. You murdered me. My own daughter. Richard isn't too happy, either. Touch Lady Margaret and you will both be sorry. You will never be free of us, so beware.

Gwendolyn stared, the terror in her eyes was chilling. Even Bessie turned away. Jenkins reached out, touching her arm, just in time to catch her as she fell, giving in to the relief of unconsciousness.

Sandra Stoner-Mitchell

*****

The door to the solicitor's business abode opened, and Miles wasted no time with polite niceties, he barged past the girl who was standing there.

'I'm here to see Mr Crankston-Smythe, and I want to see him now. Tell him Miles Brandon is here.'

Faced with Miles' commanding presence, the girl nodded and scurried off. Moments later, the solicitor came out.

'Good afternoon, Lord Brandon, I was not expecting a visit from you today.'

'No, I don't expect you were. We have things to discuss.' Miles stood at least six inches taller than the man standing in front of him. Bringing himself up to his full six foot five, he made sure the solicitor had to look up to him.

'Certainly. Come into my office.' The colour had drained from Mr Crankston-Smythe's face as he led the way along the corridor. Once in his office, he offered Miles a seat and went around his desk to sit on his own. 'What is it you wish to discuss, Lord Brandon?'

'I'll come straight to the point.' He moved over to the chair but didn't sit down. 'I want to know the exact dealings you had with my father when you fraudulently stole Lord Crawford's estate from him, making him bankrupt. Please do not test my temper, sir, by telling me you know nothing of what I'm talking about. You

The Return

see, before Lord Crawford's sudden demise, he left his wife a note.'

The solicitor was not going to fall into the same trap he had with Miles' father. He'd made a complete fool of himself that day talking about ghosts and people from the future. 'What do you know?' he asked wearily, realising he might soon be losing his freedom.

'I know he did not gamble his estate away, and I know you and my father deliberately ruined him. I want to know how you managed to convince him to part with his money. What did you offer him?'

'I didn't offer him anything. I just acted as solicitor for them both, drawing up the contracts, and plans. Lord and Lady Brandon did the rest.'

'My mother was a part of this?' Miles finally sat down, his hand rubbing his forehead. 'How on earth did my mother get involved? This sounds to me like you are trying to wiggle your way out, and pass the guilt onto others. You had better be able to prove what you are about to tell me, or you'll be in bigger trouble than you're in now.'

Beads of sweat glistened on Mr Crankston-Smythe's brow. He brought out a handkerchief and patted his forehead and cheeks. 'I don't have any physical proof of what your parents said, but you might understand what I overheard. Your mother told Lord Brandon she would not have the daughter of … of …'

'Spit it out man.' Miles' anger was building by the

second.

'I can't repeat your mother's exact words, suffice to say, she would not have you marry the daughter of … of Lady Margaret's mother. It was then the plan was hatched. Lord Brandon asked me to draw up plans for a summer resort, hotel, tennis courts, bowls, and more, at Lymington, overlooking the sea. In actual fact, the idea was good, and would have been an excellent investment. But this was never going to happen, it was all a lie, to cheat Lord Crawford out of his money in order to bankrupt him. It took a while, but in the end, your father persuaded Lord Crawford to sign a contract. Of course, Lord Crawford had me look over it for him, and … and I told him it would make him a fortune.'

Miles showed no emotion as he sat looking at the man in front of him. 'And what did you get out of this … this despicable deed? What was your share?' Miles shook his head. 'How can you sit there and call yourself a solicitor, a member of the law? Have you no shame?'

At this, Mr Crankston-Smythe sat up straight, an angry expression flooding his face. 'I will not tolerate any more criticism from you. Your family has already taken my self-respect. Shame? Yes. I've not slept well since the day I agreed to do this for your parents. Money? Ha. How much was I paid? Nothing. Absolutely nothing, not a single farthing. Your father

The Return

told me that his silence was payment enough. I have no idea what your father did with the estate, and quite honestly, I don't want to know. Your parents are ruthless, and I want nothing more to do with them.'

With that, the solicitor stood up and went over to the cupboards where he kept his files. He rummaged through until he found what he wanted, a folder. He took out a paper and handed it to Miles.

'I take it you can read Latin? Read it and look at the signatures on the bottom. And you'll see my signature and my secretary's witnessing the agreement.'

Having learnt Latin at Eton College, Miles was familiar with the legal jargon in the document. It was all there. Everything Crankston-Smythe had said, signed by his father and Lord Crawford.

30

M iles paced up and down Roger Crankston-Smythe's room, trying to get his head around all the solicitor had just told him. He'd always believed his sweet Meg's father had been weak, irresponsible, and plain selfish for using his estate to fund his gambling addiction.

Now he had proof in his hands that the gambling addiction had all been a calculated lie, instigated by his father to cover up his deliberate attempt to defraud and bankrupt Lord Crawford. To learn his mother was also involved in this swindle, had all been one hell of a shock. Miles closed his eyes. His head was pounding.

The Return

'Would you like a coffee?' the solicitor asked tentatively, trying to imagine what the man in front of him must be feeling. 'Perhaps you would prefer something stronger, a glass of whisky or brandy? Not quite the quality you're used to, but not bad.'

'What? Oh, yes, thank you. Although it's a bit early in the day for alcohol, under the circumstances, a small whisky would go down nicely.' Miles went back to the chair he'd vacated, and dropped into it.

'Look, Mr Cranston-Smythe, whilst you don't come out of this completely blameless or with your integrity intact, you could have refused to play any part in the scheme. I also know how intimidating my father can be to get his own way.'

'Please, call me Roger. I realise my name is a bit of a mouthful.'

Miles nodded. 'Roger. Then there is my mother's part in all this. The more secrets that are coming to light about her, I realise now I don't know her at all. It seems my entire life has been based on lies and pretence.'

Roger poured them both a whisky and handed a glass to Miles before taking a large swig of his own. He used the moment struggling to think of ways to repair the damage he'd helped to cause.

'If there's any way, anything I can do to help rectify this, just ask. I know I can't bring Lord Crawford back, but …' he shrugged, 'I've had this on my conscience all these years and want it out in the open. The repercussions didn't stop at bankrupting Lord Crawford. It destroyed his whole family, and resulted in Lord Crawford's suicide and the church's refusal to allow his burial in consecrated grounds.'

There was a moment when both men mulled this over; each with their own thoughts. Both angry.

'He was a good man and didn't deserve that,' Roger continued. 'Lady Crawford then suffered the added humiliation of watching her friends turn their backs on her before being forced to leave her family home.... The list goes on. All this happened because your parents didn't want you to marry Lady Margaret.'

Miles nodded. 'I know. It gets worse with every revelation. Bearing in mind this is down to my parents, I don't know what either you or I can do to put things right.'

'I kept that,' the solicitor said, as he raised his eyebrows and pointedly stared at the document lying on the table, 'more for my own protection than anything. But it's evidence you can use.'

'It's lucky for you that you did. Keep it safe. We're bound to need it later. For the moment, I have other pressing things to do. I have the unpleasant task of explaining all this to Lady Margaret. But first, I'll be paying my parents a visit.'

He stared at the glass in his hand, his mind drifting,

The Return

not wanting any of this to be true. But it was, and he must deal with it.

'I'm here if you need me to back you up, Lord Brandon. I realise I'll be struck off but I need the truth to be told.'

*****

Arriving at his family home, Miles told the butler to ask Lady Brandon to join him in Lord Brandon's study.

Lord Brandon looked up, his face flushed, ready to bark insults at the person who had just marched into the room without permission. He frowned when he saw his son standing before him.

'So, you've come crawling back, have you? Well, you needn't think for one minute that I'm going to greet you like the father of the prodigal son. I'm not the forgiving kind. What do you want?'

'Let's wait until Mother arrives.' Miles pulled the chair round ready to
accommodate his mother when she arrived. Which was quicker than he'd thought.

Lady Brandon, her face contorted with rage, stormed into the room and slammed the door behind her. 'How dare you send the butler to my room, demanding my presence as if I were a mere kitchen maid?'

'Won't you take a seat?' Miles said, as he stood by

the side of the desk and, with something like a royal wave, directed her to the chair. He then waited for her to arrange the expanse of her elegant gown as she sat, stiff and upright, glaring first at her husband, then at her son.

'Are you going to just stand there, Miles, or are you going to tell me what this is all about?'

Miles stood a moment longer, gazing at the man almost swallowed up by his leather chair. With the sun shining through the open heavy drapes onto the magnificent mahogany desk, the room screamed wealth and opulence. He couldn't help comparing all this to what Lady Crawford had stolen from her. When he turned his attention to his mother, he scowled.

'I want to know what you did with Lord Crawford's estate after you stole it,' Miles said with a calmness he wasn't feeling. 'And please, don't try blustering your way out of this. I know about the fake investment. And just so you know, I feel nothing but contempt for you both.

How dare you.' Lord Brandon leapt from his seat with fury in his eyes, just as Lady Brandon sprang from hers.

She reached up and slapped Miles across the face. 'How dare you speak to me like that? I'm your mother.' Suddenly, she let out a chilling groan, her face contorting into a grimace of pain. She clutched

The Return

her heart and fell back into her chair.

Miles stared at her with obvious disgust. 'Really? We're playing a death scene now? For heaven's sake grow up and try being honest for once in your life. I've had all the lies and deceit up to here,' he said, touching his forehead. 'It would serve you right if you genuinely did have a heart attack. As for being my mother, you gave up the right to call yourself that, years ago. You've had all the sympathy you're going to get from me.'

Ignoring his wife, Lord Brandon turned his wrath onto Miles. 'Who do you think you are bursting in here with your insults, disrespecting your parents and demanding answers to things that have nothing to do with you … I think you should leave now, and never grace my home again.'

Miles cocked an eyebrow, 'I'm going nowhere. And this has *everything* to do with me. Just because Lady Crawford rejected your advances in favour of her husband, you think you can tell me who I can and can't marry? Well, Sir, let me tell you now, I don't care what either of you think. I am marrying Lady Margaret. And if you make a fuss, I will talk to my solicitor and have you both arrested for fraud, defamation of character, and theft. And, I'd find a way of bringing a murder charge by default into it as well.'

Lord Brandon laughed. 'Just try it, and you'll see

just what I am capable of. You have no proof of any of this.'

'Oh, but I have. Lord Crawford wasn't quite as foolish as you thought. He left a letter to Lady Crawford, telling her the truth. And Mr Crankston-Smythe has some very damning documents which back up the letter Lady Margaret now has in her possession. He kept them as a precaution in case something like this happened and you put all the blame on him. I have a file of papers describing the Summer Resort you had Lord Crawford invest in. All fake, of course. I'm sure a judge would find them very interesting reading.'

Lady Branford sat up, her heart attack forgotten, as she glared at Miles. 'You say one single word, and you will be disinherited, do you understand me? You ungrateful, spiteful man. How I ended up with a son like you…'

'What happened to Lord Crawford's estate?' Miles cut in, ignoring his mother's tirade. 'If I have to leave here without knowing, I'll take it to the law. Your choice.'

The silence was deafening until Lord Brandon started drumming his fingers on the table, irritating Lady Brandon. Her face contorted with hatred. She released all the resentment she'd built up over the years.

'This is all your fault. Yours and that pathetic

woman you've been obsessed with, even after she died.'

'Shut up, woman. You're nothing but a dried up, jealous hag. Who could blame me if I *had* preferred the unattainable to what I ended up with? It was you who decided to use any means possible to stop Miles from marrying Lady Margaret. Your idea to destroy the family. All because of your insane envy. You didn't once stop to think it was your frigid attitude that had a lot to do with ruining our relationship and nothing to do with Emma.'

Miles stood there, watching, unable to take in the venomous scene playing out in front of him. 'STOP.'

Both Lord and Lady Brandon froze, suddenly realising what they were saying. They stared at Miles, knowing they could be in serious trouble.

31

Miles looked at his parents' faces. If it wasn't so serious, he would have found them quite comical. They sat like two children caught out in some misdemeanour in school. But it *was* serious. He knew it, and they did, too.

Without another word spoken, Lady Brandon stood up and marched out of the room. Father and son were left staring at each other.

'It wasn't supposed to end that way … you know, with Henry … It never once entered my head he'd go and sh——.'

'You destroyed him. How did you think it would end? You took his home away, you had Lady Crawford and Meg evicted with nowhere to go. How could you be so damned cruel?' Miles couldn't believe what he was hearing. 'All of that just because I want to marry Meg? That's beyond contempt.'

All the fight and indignation suddenly fell away from Lord Brandon. 'I'm not going to make any excuses because I don't have any to justify what we did.'

'I'm sorry, father, but that's not good enough. I can't and won't accept that you went ahead to ruin Lord Crawford simply for the hell of it. You've done some harsh things over the years, but this beats them all. I've already established you did it so you had an excuse to stop me from marrying Meg. What I want to know is, WHY? *Why* didn't you want me to marry her? What had Meg, or her family, done to you and Mother to have you financially destroy them and discredit their good name?'

Lord Brandon sighed deeply and turned away from his son's bewildered eyes. 'It goes back to the day your mother and I got married. Your grandmother naturally sent wedding invites to everyone in their circle of friends, including Henry, Emma and both sets of parents. Everything was fine until half way through the reception. Your mother overheard someone say I wanted to marry Emma, but Henry had asked her first. After that, your mother believed I'd married her on the rebound, which was total nonsense. Yes, Emma was lovely and, yes, she would have come with a large dowry, but she was in love with Henry. Okay, I was miffed, but that was all.'

Miles' father's eyes clouded as he spoke of the day so long ago that changed everything. The course of his and Elizabeth's future together had been irrevocably set.

'Your mother and I could have been happy if that blockhead had kept his mouth shut. Everything would have been different. It is most unfortunate that Meg is her mother in looks and temperament. Every time your mother saw you with her, she saw me and Emma. It drove her crazy.'

Miles stood up and walked over to the window. How stark everything looked. The few leaves clinging valiantly to the branches of the old majestic oak, had finally given up. Hypnotised, he watched them zigzagging on the air to join the carpet of orange and red leaves already covering the ground. Even disrobed, the tree retained its elegance. It was strange how similar humanity and nature were. Both can be so beautiful, yet are also capable of such devastating cruelty.

Now he tried to see this present dilemma from both sides. But it always came back to the brutal ordeal they'd put Meg and her family through. There *was* no excuse for what they'd done. He was about to say as much, but when he turned back and looked at his father, he was shocked to notice for the first time how drawn and haggard he'd become.

'What did you do with Lord Crawford's estate, Father? I want the truth. It was stolen from him. He never gambled it away, you took it. What did you do with it?'

*****

Margot told Jane that she was going to have a rest and didn't want to be disturbed. Once in the privacy of her room, Margot and Bessie went straight to the chairs by the window.

'Do you think we've stopped Meg's murder? I can't see Gwendolyn and Jenkins going through with it now, can you?'

Bessie chuckled. 'I's thinking Gwendolyn will be too busy looking out for her husband's and father's ghost to be thinking of Meg. But Meg's not out of the woods yet. Her murderer is still in the background, biding time.'

'How on earth do you know that?'

''Cause you's still in Meg's body.'

'Oh.' That reply threw her. 'I wondered what would happen when we'd saved Meg. So, is that when I go back to my own time? Meg and Miles carry on with their lives as if nothing has happened? Won't Meg be confused when I've gone?'

'I's answered that question yonks ago. You's not listening. Meg'll have the memories you's leaving in her head. But not the ones with me in them. Everything that happened with Miles, all those conversations you's shared, the picture breaking, the letters, she's gonna remember all of them as if'n it were her that lived them.'

'What if the solicitor mentions his visit by Lord Crawford's ghost? Or Gwendolyn's visitation from her late father's ghost?'

'I's thinking Meg will say what anyone would say; she'd ask them what the heck they's talking about.'

Margot thought about that. It did make sense. Who would like it spread around that they'd seen and spoken to a ghost? 'Yes, I get your point.' Then another thought hit her. 'Won't we be around to see how it all ends?'

Bessie said nothing, but the twinkle was back in her eyes, teasing Margot.

'Sometimes you're just too much, Bessie.' Margot said angrily. Then grinned. 'Okay. So, if it's not Gwendolyn and Romeo, and it's not Richard, he's right out of the picture. Who else wants Meg dead?'

Bessie cocked an eyebrow. 'Well…. I's thinking it's most likely to be Lord Brandon. He's the one who's been shouting his head off about not wanting his son to marry Meg. We's can be pretty sure why and all. *And* we's can bring in Lady Brandon after what I's happened to be overhearing.'

'Mmm, but isn't she a bit too old to be going around

killing people?' Margot was more than a little sceptical.

'What's age got to do with it? All she needs is a knife, which she'd find in their kitchen. I's sure the cook would keep 'em nice and sharp. It don't take much effort to cut through a bit of leather with the right tool.'

Of course, Bessie was right, *again*. Although Margot hadn't met the lady yet, from what she'd heard about her, Lady Brandon would be more than capable. 'Okay, so where do we go from here?'

'I's not knowing for the minute.' Bessie stared into the distance. It was one of those looks that had Margot wishing she could get inside her friend's head. 'I's *am* knowing that we's not got much time left.'

That brought Margot up with a start. 'Crikey, you're right. I wonder if Miles

read those letters and documents you left on the step … Oh. I just had a thought … How should I react when Miles tells me what we already know? How would Meg react? I know how I'd feel if someone told me that my father had been defrauded of all he owned; that it was the father of my fiancé who had deliberately set out to destroy *my* entire family, *and* succeeded. I'd go ballistic.'

Margot and Bessie gawped at each other; it was obvious neither of them had given this a thought.

'I's thinking you's got to tread carefully. I's also

thinking that Miles is going to be in a state, too. He's got to tell his beloved Meg.'

'What a mess. I feel so sorry for both of them. Meg, because of what happened   to her parents, and Miles, because it was his parents who were responsible. This will be the hardest part of this assignment. I'm not sure how to deal with it.'

'We's gonna find out soon enough.' Bessie was looking out the window. 'Miles has just put his horse in the stable.'

Margot leaned over to look for herself. 'Oh dear. He doesn't look very happy, does he? Look, if you think of something to help me with this, please tell me.'

Bessie nodded. 'Course. For now, I's thinking you's should go and meet him and see what he has to say, and I'll listen in.'

Margot checked her hair in the mirror, and pinched her cheeks to put some colour in them. Then, after smoothing her skirts, she made her way down the stairs just in time to greet Miles as he came through the door.

'Miles. Is everything alright? You look so miserable ... has something happened?' She rushed up to him. Her concern was genuine, more so when he pulled her into his arms. He was hugging her so tight; she could barely breathe. It was as if this would be the last time she'd see him. Whatever else he'd learned, she knew this was going to be as difficult for him as it would be for her.

The Return

'You smell nice,' he told her, nuzzling her neck.
'Let's go and sit down. I have a lot to tell you, not all of it good.'

They walked into the sitting room, and Meg suggested some refreshment, wanting to put off the dreaded moment.

'We have some home-made ginger beer, if you'd like a glass. Apparently, Cook was shown how to make it a few months ago, and gave me a glass to try yesterday. It's delicious and very refreshing.'

'I've tried it, and yes, it is refreshing.'

Margot left the room to find Jane, giving herself a moment to compose herself. This wasn't going to be easy.

32

Miles leapt to his feet when the sitting room door opened and Margot came back in. He was startled to discover how apprehensive he felt. Having had a few moments to go over in his mind what he had to say, it was hardly surprising he was worried.

'Mary will bring our refreshments in shortly,' Margot told him, with a smile that squeezed his heart. 'In the meantime, let's sit down and you can tell me what's giving you that funny scowl. You mentioned having good and bad news. I'm not sure which I prefer to hear first. Will you decide for me, Miles?'

Miles smiled, but only because it was hard not to

The Return

when he was facing the love of his life. He looked at her now, the lady he had adored for so long. It felt as

if he'd loved her his whole life. His mind travelled back to the evening he first laid eyes on Meg.

One minute he was a happy, carefree bachelor, talking to a friend at a lavish dinner party; the next, he glanced across the room and his whole world flipped up and over, never to be the same again.

His eyes were transfixed by the sight of stunning flame-red hair, falling in a mass of curls, and leaving him desperate to run his fingers through them. He couldn't understand why he'd never seen her before. Why hadn't his parents ever invited her family to their parties? Those questions could wait. For now, all he wanted was to see the face that owned those gorgeous locks.

Determined to find out, he began to weave his way through the other guests. He had barely made it half-way across the room when she turned. Their eyes locked. His breath caught in his throat. His heart raced. He felt like a school kid with a crush on his teacher.

Now he could see the whole picture, he was smitten, entranced. Those gorgeous fiery locks framed the most adorable face, with its cute little nose, speckled with freckles. Without knowing anything about her, he knew he was in love, a condition that controlled every nerve-ending in his body, and one from which he never wished to recover.

His heart ached as he realised it was all about to end. He'd never felt so wretched. Now Meg was searching his face, waiting for an answer.

'Miles? What do you think I should hear first?'

'Parhaps I should start where I've been told it all began. My parents' wedding day.'

Margot sat and listened, not interrupting once. Her eyes flickered towards Bessie a few times, as more details were divulged which they'd known nothing about. It was such a tragic story; Margot could feel her eyes misting up.

Mistaking them to be tears of anguish, Miles pulled her into his arms. 'Saying sorry, is simply not enough but, to my eternal shame, it's all I have, my love. My parents are responsible for your father's death, and your mother's despair at losing him along with everything else she held dear. Nothing I can say or do will right that wrong. I'd give my life to be able to turn the clock back … I would quite understand if your feelings for me have changed and … and you don't want to see me again.'

Gently pushing away, Margot took in Miles' distraught features, and the agony in his eyes. She brought her hand up and touched his face. 'None of what happened was your fault, Miles. My parents would be the first to agree with me. I know you.

The Return

You're a kind, gentle, loving man. My feelings for you could never change, any more than yours did for me after my father's suicide and subsequent loss of his fortune. I love you with all my heart and always will. No one could ever destroy that.' As she said it, Margot knew it was true, she would always love him. 'Please, will you finish the story?'

'There isn't much more to tell, only that so many lives were ruined by an unfortunate comment at my parents' wedding. If my mother had only listened to my father, and believed him, perhaps none of this would have happened. But she didn't. And because of that, you and your entire family were forced to suffer the most malicious attack of lies and humiliation that was in her power to inflict upon you.' Miles stopped, searching Meg's face. 'Do you have a picture of your mother as a young woman?'

'Yes, I do. It's small.' Margot removed the locket hanging around her neck. She'd opened it the day after taking over Meg's body, thinking it was the one she'd seen of Meg and Miles in her own time. But these were miniature photos of Lord and Lady Crawford. Margot had been surprised at the similarity between Meg's mother and her own. 'This was taken on her wedding day.'

Miles took it and frowned as he concentrated on the photos. He then returned his attention to Margot.'

'This could easily be a picture of you.'

Sandra Stoner-Mitchell

'Mother was prettier than me,' Margot said softly, her voice trembling a little as she thought of her own mother who had died recently, then sighed. 'All this grief and misery because your mother wouldn't accept your father's word. It not only ruined her own life, she made sure others suffered, too. What your parents did to my family, … I'm not sure if I can forgive them. At least, I'm not ready to yet. What they did was beyond cruel, it was vindictive and unconscionable. I lost my father. He was a good, gentle man. And I believe I lost my mother much too early because of it. Our lives could have been so different … all our lives. We were soon to be one big family. Why did your father go along with her plans? Do you know?'

Miles shook his head. 'I never thought to ask, but I will. Maybe he thought it was a way to appease Mother, although that would be a first. I've never seen him try before, or been witness to the smallest display of affection between them. At their ages, I'm sure all this bitterness is hard to cope with, but they've lived with it far too long to be able to change. If that had been his reason, it was never going to happen. After all these years, if there had been any love there, it's all gone now. The problem was, I believe, once he started the campaign to ruin your father, there was no way he could stop without ruining his own reputation. I think that's why he did nothing about your family home.'

'What do you mean?' Margot was extremely interested in this part. From the corner of her eye, she was aware of movement. Without looking, she knew Bessie's ears would have pricked up at the mention of the Crawford's manor house. She was as curious as Margot to discover what Miles had learned.

'This is the good news. He never sold it. Apparently, he has kept all the staff your parents employed, insisting they continue to maintain it in the way your mother liked it. Although he never said, and quite honestly, I don't believe he would own up to it, I do believe when *your* father died, mine suffered an acute influx of guilt. Deservedly so. Although, he still had to keep us apart or his life would be worse than it is now.'

Miles looked into Margot's eyes. 'This doesn't mean you and I won't ever get married … if you will still have me, of course? No, don't answer that yet. I want you to be sure. Think over all I've told you, and then decide.'

He waited until Margot agreed, then continued. 'From what I've learned, my parents are not the people they were before they married. The bitterness, the lies and the distrust has irrevocably changed them. Before I came here, I went to see your family home. I might have got ahead of myself, but I've told them to expect their Mistress back and to get the rooms prepared. It's yours, Meg, you can move in whenever you want.'

Margot stared at Bessie, and raised a questioning eyebrow.

'I's thinking you's has to go there. It's Meg's home, and it will be where Miles and Meg will live once they's married.'

Margot considered carefully how Meg might feel. Believing she and Meg were similar in almost every respect, she couldn't help but presume she'd know her thoughts now. 'I think that before I decide to move back, I'd like to visit first … I'm worried I'll be haunted by what happened … at the end.'

Miles closed his eyes. He'd not given that a thought. 'I'm such a fool. I'm sorry, my love. Of course you would be apprehensive. Anyone would be. Tell me when you want to visit, and I'll take you.'

'How about now? I don't want time to think about it. Can you take me now?'

'Go and get your coat, while I get your carriage brought around to the door.'

Margot gave Bessie a 'follow me' look and went up to her room. As soon as Bessie was inside, Margot closed the door.

'I think this is how Meg would play it. Whilst she has many happy memories there, what happened with her father, and the subsequent eviction of her mother, must still be quite raw.'

The Return

'I's thinking you's be right. There might be a problem with some of the staff. You's were born and grew up in that house, and some will remember the friendship you had with them.'

The smile on Margot's face slipped. 'Oh no. I don't want to make the same mistake as I did with Lucy. That could have been disastrous had you not told me in time. Perhaps Miles could mention that this is my first visit, and I need privacy, or something like that.'

'Good idea. But I's'll be there if'n you's needing me.'

Margot looked at the lady she'd known for such a short while, yet had become more than a friend to her. On impulse, she threw her arms around Bessie and hugged her tight, then went to get her coat, leaving Bessie looking astonished.

*****

Miles went up the steps to the main door of the Crawford's manor house, and knocked. When the butler answered, Margot watched as Miles spoke to him. The butler looked towards the coach, then nodded. Leaving the door open, he walked off, and Miles went to help Margot down from the coach.

'You won't be disturbed while you look around. If you prefer, I'll stay outside and wait.'

Margot was quick to dismiss such an idea, and told

him so. 'We'll go together.'

The manor had been kept beautifully. She could see her own mother furnishing it the way Meg's had. Margot moved from room to room, careful not to say anything in case she gave herself away.

All was going well until they reached *the* door. Bessie had mention it was Lord Crawford's study. A sense of dread engulfed her. A coldness swept over her, and she started shaking. She knew this was affecting Meg, not her.

Miles could see Margot shaking and, reaching out, took her hand off the doorknob. 'You don't have to go in there, Meg. Leave this room, with all its horrors, locked away.'

Margot had the weirdest feeling that she had to go inside, that Meg wanted her to. She looked up into Miles' eyes, and smiled. 'No, this is something I have to do, if I want to come back.'

Miles dropped her hand, but didn't argue. 'If you find it difficult, come straight out.'

She nodded and immediately turned to the door, and took a deep breath.

The Return

33

Before entering Lord Crawford's study, Margot turned her head to look at Miles. Worry lines were etched into his face. She knew his reservations about her going in were sound, but all the same, he respected her wishes and stood aside. She smiled, gently reaching out to touch his hand.

'I'll be fine, Miles. I can't begin to explain it, but I *need* to do this … alone.' Margot couldn't understand this ridiculous compulsion herself, let alone explain it to this man she'd fallen hopelessly in love with. 'I promise not to stay inside for long.' She smiled once more, hoping to allay his fears, but knowing it wouldn't.

The first thing Margot noticed as the door slowly swung open was the awful smell. Her nose wrinkled in distaste. The walls were permeated from years of pipe-smoking and cigars, leaving the room with such an appalling stench, she could almost taste it. But having come this far, she was determined to see it through.

Although Margot didn't know what the *it* was, she would bet a week's wages Meg did. Somehow, Meg was the controlling force now, and it was she who wanted to enter. Margot continued in and shut the door behind her. Now it was closed, the smell seemed to increase. 'Crikey, what a stink.'

'It's not nice,' Bessie agreed, as she tilted her head back and sniffed loudly. 'I's wondering how it can hang around for so long. It's been years since anyone's come in here. I's knowing for a fact the staff haven't. Most are scared. They's thinking Lord Crawford's ghost is still sitting in his chair. Superstitious nonsense.'

'What? How can you even say that?' Margot shook her head. Sometimes Bessie was more than a little weird. 'Anyway, I guess that's why it stinks so much. Apart from the smell, it's also stuffy in here, I doubt the window has been opened in years. Let's rectify that and let some fresh air in.' She went over and was about to pull the curtain, when, without warning, her arm was pulled back and she was made to walk over to Lord Crawford's desk. *This gets freakier by the second.*

The Return

She glanced back and saw Bessie's perplexed frown at the sudden change, and shrugged. 'It's not my doing.'

Then using only her index finger, she lightly brushed the desk. She wasn't at all surprised when, like the previous times, Margot was shown a scene that happened over one hundred years before she was born. This time, it was nothing as glamorous as wearing a ball gown or a wedding dress. This time, it was the aftermath of Lord Crawford's suicide.

Lord Crawford was sitting at his desk, bent forward with his face laid on the blotting pad, and a gaping hole in the top of his head. The sight of so much blood everywhere was horrifying. He'd clearly held the gun under his chin and fired. The scene was unlike anything Margot had ever seen, and hoped she never would again. She didn't know whether to scream or throw up. She did know she wished Meg hadn't wanted to come here.

Her attention was taken from the grim, stomach-churning scene, when a distraught Lady Crawford burst through the door. She instantly took in what had happened and screamed as she staggered towards the desk. Margot wanted so much to comfort her but, knowing she was invisible in her visions, she could only watch the events unfold.

Lady Crawford edged around the desk and, lifting her husband's head, she cradled it in her arms.

Oblivious to the blood covering her bodice, she tenderly moved his hair, trying to cover the gaping hole. Her tears were left to run unchecked as she quietly whimpered and lamented her loss.

Within moments of hearing Lady Crawford scream, members of her staff came rushing in. Upon witnessing the horrific scene, one maid ran back out and threw up in the hall. The rest of them stood and stared, unable to register what they were seeing. It was only when Meg rushed in that they managed to pull themselves together. While some made way for her, others tried to stop her going any further. She shook them off.

Meg stood stock-still, looking at her mother then at her father. She didn't cry out, or rush to her mother's side. Her eyes were fixated on her father's head. Those still standing around, could only look on as the realisation of her father's death slowly sank in. Meg's face drained of colour; her mouth opened but she made no sound. Margot could tell the young woman was in shock. She'd need time and gentle handling to help her through this trauma.

One of the servants put her arm around Meg's waist and led her out of the room. Another went up to Lady Crawford, and gently pulled her away. It was then she spotted the note that Margot would later find in the book.

Leaning over to pick it up, Lady Crawford tucked

The Return

it in her pocket, then allowed herself to be taken away.

The scene faded; Margot was back with Bessie. But before she could repeat what she'd seen, things went crazy. It was pitch black, so black she couldn't even see her hands. Fear rushed in, supplanting common-sense. Margot was falling into an endless dark void. Panic-stricken, her arms flailed as she tried to save herself. She called Bessie's name, but there was no answer. Then, as suddenly as it started, it ended.

Margot closed her eyes, waiting until everything stopped spinning. When she opened them, she found herself facing the mirror. Except, she was still standing in the middle of Lord Crawford's study, and there was no mirror … It was Meg.

The women stood facing each other, open-mouthed, their eyes saucer-wide in surprise, until Margot blinked and turned to Bessie, hoping for an explanation.

But Bessie looked just as surprised. She stared from Margot to Meg and back again.

Margot guessed Bessie was in just as much turmoil as she was. She had never expected something like this to happen. Meg had started inching backwards towards the door and that would not be good. Margot had to think fast.

'I don't think this should be happening. How did you manage to force me out of you?'

Meg looked frightened. It was obvious to both Margot and Bessie that she didn't have a clue about what had just happened. 'What do you mean, force you out of me?'

Bessie had pulled herself together and now stepped in. 'Hello Meg, I's knowing all this is a· mite confusing, but can you tell us what was the last thing you remember?'

Meg stood quietly for a moment, trying to focus her mind. 'Miles didn't want me to come in here, but I knew I must.' She turned her head and looked around. 'This is where Father…. I haven't been in this room since…' Meg took a deep breath. Margot and Bessie didn't rush her. This had to be very hard.

'I remember touching the doorknob and … it was like I'd been struck by lightning. I was in here, staring at my father. How could that be? Who are you? What is happening to me? Miles. I want Miles.'

Margot didn't have time to explain. 'Look, we need to talk, but not yet. Miles is standing outside this door, waiting for you to come back out. He's worried you'll get hurt again. I think it might be a good idea if Bessie tells you what's going on, and why we have to keep this pretence up for a little while longer. I'll get Miles to continue showing me around your mansion.' Margot was about to go back to Miles, when she stopped to face Meg again.

'This is just a thought. I told Miles that I wanted to

The Return

see if I would feel comfortable coming back to live here again. After what happened here … do you want to move back? All your staff are still here. How do you feel about it?'

Meg was looking quite angry now. 'I said that to Miles ... Not you.'

Bessie nodded. 'That's right, you did.' She turned to Margot, and winked.

'I's thinking you should go to Miles, and carry on as you's were. Meg and I's'll have a little chat while you's away.'

Margot nodded, and opened the door. It was then she realised that now she was out of Meg's body, Miles couldn't see her. He didn't move, just looked through her to Meg.

Love and worry were intermingled in his voice. 'Are you okay? Shall we move on now?'

Margot could have wept. How she wanted him to be looking at her like that. How she wanted to feel his arms around her one more time. The sudden thought that she would never sleep with him again, feel his hands on her body.

…. *How can I carry on seeing him and not hold him? Not be able to touch him?*

Margot was hyperventilating. She tried to calm herself by deep-breathing. She'd heard somewhere that it could help. She didn't believe it, but tried anyway.

Sandra Stoner-Mitchell

It was then she noticed Meg staring at her, and swallowed hard. The question in her eyes was clear. She had noticed Miles hadn't seen her, and was unsure what to do.

Margot gave a feeble smile, and with one last deep breath, said. 'I think you must go with him. Bessie and I will come to you when you are on your own and answer your questions. Be careful, though. You mustn't mention us.'

With barely a nod, Meg walked out to Miles. Just before the door closed, Margot saw Meg wrapped in Miles arms. The pain that engulfed her was so intense it felt almost physical. In that moment a part of her died.

Bessie came to her, and patted her arm. 'Meg and Miles will carry on as before. Now you are out of her body, all you've done with Miles are now her memories. I's thinking you's gonna be fine. Come on, we's got things to do.'

Margot wanted to scream at Bessie. *How can I be fine? My soulmate just walked away with another woman in his arms.* But, of course, she couldn't do that. It wasn't Bessie's fault. Margot knew what she'd been getting into, *and* she'd said she wanted to help. But when she said that, she had no idea she would fall hopelessly in love with Miles.

She looked at Bessie, and nodded. 'Okay, what do we do next?'

The Return

'Well, we's got to get a plan two. Now you's left Meg, we's gotta think of how we's gonna get Meg to help us catch her murderer. Her death is supposed to happen the day after tomorrow.'

34

After watching Miles leave the following morning, Margot and Bessie waited a few minutes before walking around to the back of the house. They passed Jane, the kitchen maid, who looked to be in a world of her own as she threw bacon-fat and bread out for the birds.

She'd left the kitchen door ajar. Bessie peeped in before opening it wider, just in case anyone was there who'd notice. Walking through the kitchen, they could hear Cook muttering away to herself in the large walk-in pantry, while another kitchen maid was tackling the washing up.

Bessie walked over to the dining room, and came back to report that Meg wasn't there. 'I's thinking that

The Return

she might have gone up to her room. Let's find out.'

Margot tapped on Meg's bedroom door and, hearing the call to enter, she and Bessie went in. Meg was sitting by the window, and even in her own misery, Margot had to stifle a smile when she saw the fleeting look of confusion in Meg's eyes. Of course, meeting your doppelganger had to be a tad disconcerting, Margot could affirm that, and was thankful she'd passed that stage now.

Bessie walked straight over to sit on the only other chair in the room, leaving Margot to sit on the bed. The bed she had recently slept in; where Miles had brought her body to a writhing crescendo of exquisite, breath-taking pleasure.

Margot closed her eyes and breathed deeply. *How am I going to live without you, Miles? What will I do?* She felt her eyes moisten. Clenching her hands into fists, digging her nails into her skin, she willed the physical pain to drive away the emotional trauma of loss. But nothing helped.

Blinking rapidly, Margot came back to the present just in time to hear Bessie open the conversation.

'I's thinking you's got a lot of questions to ask so I's gonna get straight to the point. I's needing you to listen to what we's got to tell you with an open mind. It will save a lot of time … and time, my dear, is something we's fast running out of. Margot here will be able to tell it better'n me. Okay?'

Meg nodded, but didn't say a word. She turned to look at Margot, who smiled, noting her confusion had changed to wariness. Margot could see Meg didn't trust her so she'd need to tread carefully.

'How did you feel being back in the manor house?' she asked, thinking to proceed with something that might put her at her ease. 'I expect it felt quite strange after all those years away.'

'It did. But it was comforting to have Miles walk beside me,' she answered. 'It also helped with my decision to move back. Although the distress my dear mother and I suffered after my father's ... death, can never be erased, I shared so many happy times with him that, if I need to, I can lean heavily on those memories to see me through.'

'That's a positive way of looking at it. One that will undoubtedly work,' Margot told her.

Margot's comments had reassured Meg somewhat and, with a bit more animation in her voice, she said 'I've already arranged to have my things taken over. When Miles and I are married we'll be living there so I might as well move back now.'

Margot took note of the slight emphasis on Miles and her upcoming marriage, but didn't rise to it. She regretted what she needed to say next but she smiled, saying 'That's a good idea. But now we have to talk to you about your future.'

Meg shifted uneasily in her chair. 'I knew there

had to be a reason. It's not every day you come face to face with yourself. What does my future have to do with anything?'

'Look, there's no easy way to put this, Meg, and I doubt very much you'll believe what I have to tell you. I totally understand that. First, I am not from your time, I'm from more than a hundred years in the future. And, secondly, Bessie came to me asking for my help to stop your murder.'

Meg stared at her, incredulous. 'My murder. Really? Are you mad? Well, I can tell you one thing you've got right, and that is, I *don't* believe you. What you are suggesting is total fantasy.' Meg started laughing. 'Anyway, why would anyone want to murder me?'

'That's what we are here to find out, and to stop it from happening. Look, Meg, I know it all sounds nonsense to you, but it's not. What I'm telling you is fact. If I'm lying, can you tell me why you can see us, but no one else can? Did Miles see us? No. Whether you believe it or not, is immaterial. Bessie and I are here to stop your murder, and we will. At the moment, we don't know who the culprit is, and we don't really have any suspects. Those we had, we've now taken off our list of possibilities. Can you think of anyone who would want you dead?'

Meg shook her head. She stared at Margot, then Bessie. She could see they were serious. And she couldn't argue that Miles couldn't see them. A ripple of fear showed on her face. 'If it *is* true, and I'll have to take your word for it, when am I supposed to die?'

'Let's get one thing straight. You are not going to die. We might not know who is going to do it … I'll rephrase that, who is going to *try* and do it, but we do know when and how, which gives us the advantage. We'll be waiting, ready to pounce, long before the person comes.'

Meg was quiet. It was a lot to take in. 'Okay, I'll go along with that. I don't want to die. So, when will this all take place? You haven't said, yet.'

Margot looked over at Bessie, who shrugged. Margot rolled her eyes. *Thanks a lot.*

'Look, you won't die. I promise you … we both promise you.' Margot took another deep breath. *Dear God, give me the strength to see this through.* 'It's supposed to happen tomorrow.'

'Tomorrow?' Meg's face paled. 'But it can't. I'm going hunting. And I'm getting married soon.' She paused, and looked at Bessie, then Margot. She grimaced. Then the absurdity of her remark hit her and she said 'That sounded ridiculous, didn't it?' A small smile played around her lips and, the next instant, she was laughing. Within seconds, Margot and Bessie had joined in the raucous laughter, and all felt the pent-up tension drain away.

'So, what's the plan?' Meg asked, when they'd

calmed down again.

'Bessie and I will be watching to see who goes into the stable and tampers with your saddle. We know the girth strap was cut, and that made it slip. You fell when your horse jumped a gate.'

There was silence for a moment as they each thought about what Margot had just said. Then Meg stood up and moved around the room, head down, deep in thought.

'I would have said it was impossible. Whoever does this would have to do it after the saddle was put on. And even then, the horse would have had to be left alone for whoever it is to get near it. *That* wouldn't happen.'

'You're right. So that means … What *does* that mean, Bessie? Because I don't
have a clue.' Margot jumped off the bed and joined Meg walking around the room until Bessie shouted at them.

'I's thinking if'n you don't sit down and stop making my eyes roll around my head, I's gonna go mad. It's just as well you's both wearing different clothes or I's be having trouble working out who's who.'

Meg returned to her chair, while Margot walked over to stare out of the window. 'I don't think we can make any sort of plan other than be there and play it by ear. Just a thought, though, who knows you're going riding tomorrow?'

'Everyone, I expect. It's the fox hunt tomorrow. Now that they realise I'm still with Miles, I've been invited to join them. We'll all meet up in the market square at ten in the morning.'

'Well, that narrows it down a bit.' Margot laughed. 'But at least we know when, so whoever it is, will arrive early. What time will you leave here?'

'Half past nine.'

'That's good. Bessie and I will be waiting for our visitor long before that. You make sure you're ready to go and watch for our signal … What signal will you give her?' Margot asked Bessie.

'I's thinking we's can shout out for Meg to come. No one else can see or hear us.'

'Good thinking. I'll yell my head off. You be waiting near the door, Meg, so you can hear me.'

'If it wasn't for the fact that someone wants to kill me, this would be quite exciting.'

*****

The following morning, Bessie and Margot climbed down from the hay bales at the far end of the stable, and went over to watch the lad get Meg's horse ready.

'You wait here and keep watch, and I'll go and see if Meg is up,' Margot said. 'We don't want anything to go wrong now.'

The Return

'I's thinking she's right by the door already.' Bessie flicked her head towards the house. 'I's thinking she's enjoying this.'

Margot looked over and, seeing Meg, she waved and gave a thumbs up.

It wasn't long before a lady in a hooded cloak came up to speak with the lad, telling him that Cook wanted to see him in the kitchen. The lad frowned and turned to Meg's horse.

'Don't worry, I'll stay here until Lady Margaret comes out.' Neither Bessie nor Margot could see who she was, the hood almost covering her face, but her voice … there was something vaguely familiar about it. Margot shook her head. When the lad still seemed reluctant, the request was made more sternly.

Once on her own, they watched as she pulled a knife from under her cloak. Margot dashed out, running and screaming loudly, calling Meg to come now.

Meg left the door open as she came quietly up to the stable. She was in time to see the knife slicing into the girth strap.

'What do you think you're doing?' Meg said, her voice icy cold.

Startled, the woman dropped the knife, and turned. Meg dashed up to her and, pulling the woman's hood down, she flinched. 'You!'

35

'Why, Lucy? I thought you were my friend! What have I ever done to make you want to kill me?' Meg was near to tears with the shock of discovering it was her best friend.

'Your friend? Your *friend?*' Lucy spat out the words as her face twisted with hatred. 'I was never your friend. You flatter yourself. The only reason I pretended to like you was to be near Miles. You knew I loved him, but you just had to make him yours, didn't you? It made me sick to watch you clinging like a limpet to his arm, showering him with those stupid love-sick eyes. Do you know how ridiculous you looked at your party?'

'I did no such thing! What is the matter with you? You've never shown any interest in Miles,' Meg was astounded at Lucy's outburst.

'It was at *my* party you met him. Didn't that tell you something?' She stopped and looked around. 'Is he still here? Or did he have to sneak out before anyone saw him? Have you no shame? Didn't you know that men don't wed the girls that readily open their legs for them? Whatever decency was left in your family, you've wiped it all away. I expect he paid for your body with this house. You sold yourself cheaply....'

Rage filled Meg's eyes, and in one fast motion, she slapped Lucy hard across the face, sending her stumbling to the ground.

'I hate you!' Lucy screeched. 'Why didn't you go into service like you were supposed to? Be a governess. Miles would have forgotten you and he would have been mine. All these years I've been seeing him, trying to make him notice me, and not once did he mention you! When he told me he was going to bring you back into society on your birthday, and throw a grand ball for the event, I was so furious, I wanted to kill *him*! But I could only pretend to be pleased and walk away.'

'I'm sorry, Lucy. But pretending to be my friend was two-faced and, quite frankly, despicable of you. Perhaps if you had been honest, and not so fixated on Miles, you might have found someone who did love you, and who you could have loved.' Meg refused to take on board any feeling of guilt or shame.

But Lucy wasn't listening, she was beyond that. She carried on as if Meg hadn't spoken. 'When I heard you were joining the hunt this year, it was like I was being given a sign from the gods! I could be rid of you altogether!' Her voice was getting louder and more excitable as all the anger and bitterness she'd nurtured came to the fore.

Margot and Bessie could only stand and watch the scene with amazement as Lucy's eyes brightened in a sudden frenzy of madness. When Lucy rolled over, stretching her arm towards the knife she'd dropped, Margot knew, without a doubt, what was in the woman's mind. Lucy intended to kill Meg regardless of the consequences.

That was not going to happen, not if she and Bessie had their way. Margot leapt forward and put her foot on it. When Lucy tried to pick the knife up, it wouldn't move. Try as she might, she couldn't get her fingers underneath it.

Just as she howled with rage, Miles galloped up to the stable and leapt off his horse. 'What's going on?'

Miles looked at Lucy, as she lay on the ground. The clips holding her hair in place had come loose and untidy locks fell over her face - a face full of fury.

His eyes took in the knife she was reaching for, and he turned to Meg, whose silent tears and pain-filled eyes, cut him to the quick. He pulled her into his arms. 'What happened, love?'

Lucy was shocked to see Miles, and quickly changed her expression to one of pain, bringing her hand up to rub her face. 'She hit me, Miles. Look!'

She struggled to her feet, marching up and presenting her reddening cheek to him. 'I thought she was my best friend.' Lucy managed to bring the tears on, adding a look of bewilderment to give credence to her story.

Miles looked at Lucy's face. The redness showed clearly. 'Meg? What happened? I don't for one minute think you would do something like that without good reason. What was it?'

'I caught her cutting the girth strap.' Meg told him, her voice trembling with confusion and hurt.

'She's lying, I did no such thing! You know me, Miles. I wouldn't do such a wicked thing. Who are you going to believe, Miles? The daughter of a cheating gambler, or me?'

Miles went over to Meg's horse and lifted the stirrup. Seeing the cuts in the girth, he turned to look at Lucy. An angry scowl filled his face. 'Are you telling me that Meg did this to her own saddle?'

'Well, I didn't do it!' Lucy sniffed. Seeing Miles did not believe her, she thought fast. 'Perhaps it was the lad who was here when I arrived.'

'Where is he?' Miles asked Meg. 'He knows he's not supposed to leave your horse saddled like this and unattended.'

'I's thinking Miles should talk to the lad, Meg,' Bessie said, walking over to her side. 'I's hearing this so-called friend of yours were speaking to him. She said Cook was wanting to see him.'

'I think I saw him going towards the kitchen,' Meg said. She turned towards the house and saw the stable-boy returning. 'There he is.'

'Jack! Get yourself over here and be quick about it!' Miles shouted. When the lad reached him, Miles eyed him sternly. 'Why did you leave Lady Margaret's horse unattended? You know that is not allowed. Make sure you tell me the truth now, or I can promise you, you'll be looking for another job.'

Jack's lip trembled, and Margot, wishing she was visible, ached to put Miles right.

The lad looked around and spotted Lucy. 'I were told by that lady there that Cook wanted t' see me. I said I couldn't go an' leave the 'orse. She tells me I 'ad t' go an' she'd stay till Lady Margaret arrived. When I got t' the kitchen, Cook didn't know what I were on about!'

'I told you no such thing! How dare you tell lies to Lord Brandon? Miles, you should get rid of him. You seem to be surrounding yourself with liars!' Lucy was now at her wits' end. As she saw the look that passed over Miles' face, she fumed. 'Well? Are you going to take the word of a stable-lad and... and your mistress?'

Miles was about to lose his temper altogether. 'I think you should go before I do something I might regret, Lucy. And need I add, don't you come anywhere near Lady Margaret again. If she has any sort of an accident, I will be after you. Do you understand what I'm saying?'

Margot had just about had enough of Lucy's nonsense. She winked at Bessie then, walking over to stand behind Lucy, she put her hands around Lucy's neck and squeezed. Meg's eyes widened as she watched.

A shrill scream ripped through the air, as Lucy began flailing her arms about, trying to get Margot's hands off her. 'Miles, help me,' she gasped. 'Don't just stand there! I'm ... I'm being strangled!'

Margot laughed and gave her a gentle push before going back to stand with Bessie.

Lucy spun around, looking for her strangler. Of course, there was no one there. Bessie and Margot were laughing, and Meg, recognising Margot's antics as

The Return

buffoonery, was trying hard now to keep a straight face.

'Go home, Lucy.' Miles was fast losing patience with her. 'Where is your carriage? Or your horse? I take it you didn't walk?'

'As if you care. I rode my horse.' She walked out of the stable, deliberately bumping into Meg as she passed.

After she'd gone, Meg turned to Miles. 'She loves you. That's why she wanted me out the way. I never knew. She never said. She seemed to think I did know and that I deliberately made sure she would never have you.'

Miles had a playful grin on his face, his eyes twinkled. 'Aha! So, my sweet Meg is really the wicked witch who cast a spell on me!' Then laughing he lifted her up and held her tight. 'Oh, Meg, I can't wait to make you Lady Brandon.' He kissed her passionately before putting her down. 'Come on, before I start wanting my devilish way with you, we have a hunt to attend. If we're not careful, we're going to be late!'

He turned to Jack, who had been standing there frightened he'd lose his job. 'Jack, get another saddle and put it on Lady Margaret's horse. I can't have her risking her life with that one now.'

'Yes, Sir!' Jack grinned and dashed off to get the other saddle, a much happier lad than he was a few minutes ago.

Miles and Meg moved out of the stable and started towards the house when Meg stopped. She turned, staring back with a puzzled frown.

'What is it?' Miles looked back too but, seeing nothing he hugged her close. 'Come, my love. Lucy's gone. No one's going to harm you now.'

Meg gave a weak smile, glanced back one last time, then took a deep breath and walked away with Miles.

Margot looked at Bessie. 'She couldn't see us, could she?'

'No, you's done your job. Meg is not going to die. She has already forgotten us. We's can leave her now.'

Margot's stomach churned; her heart ached. Not seeing Miles again … *What am I going to do?*

'What about Gwendolyn and her butler? And what about the solicitor, Miles' parents, what happens with them? Surely, they don't all get off scot-free?'

'I's thinking that's not our problem now. We's not here and as far as history's concerned, we's never were. Meg will remember all about Gwendolyn and Jenkins, and Miles won't forget what his parents and Mr Crankston-Smythe did. They's got a lot to answer for, and they will. I's thinking it's time to get you home.'

Margot wanted to argue; she wanted to stay and see what happened, but then Bessie touched her shoulder, and everything went black.…

36

Margot was kneeling on the ground, head down and feeling wretched. She kept her eyes closed, fighting the waves of nausea that washed over her, painfully aware of her thumping headache. She wanted to cry, but the tears refused to come.

She stayed still, scarcely daring to breathe. She waited until the light-headedness eased before lifting her eyelids a little. A faint sob escaped. Margot closed her eyes tight as a rush of despair swept through her. She was back in the cemetery where it all began.

She held onto the headstone in front of her, and pulled herself up. Still a bit dizzy, Margot waited for the church to stop swaying before moving again. Then, satisfied she wouldn't fall over, she stood up straight and looked about. The cemetery appeared to be empty.

'Bessie.' Margot whispered the name, and turned full circle this time, but Bessie wasn't there. Margot lowered her eyes, her heart heavy with the loss of Miles and Bessie. It was then she realised she'd been holding on to Miles' headstone. Curious, she walked over to the one beside it.

Lady Margaret Brandon

28-10-1857 — 16-5-1938

Beloved wife of Lord Miles James Brandon

Mother of Lord James Arthur Brandon

R.I.P.

'They had a son.' Margot's legs almost gave out.

'Yes, they's had a bonnie lad, thanks to you.'

Margot spun round and, with a huge smile plastered over her face, she rushed over and wrapped her arms around her friend. 'Bessie. I'm so pleased to see you. I thought you'd stayed there.'

'I's not that easy to get rid of, not when I's thinking of getting another one of you's nice cups of coffee.' Bessie chuckled. 'And I's thinking you's got some questions for me.' She raised her eyebrows, and tilted her head, revealing eyes that were twinkling a lot more than usual.

'Yes, I have. Plenty, in fact. What did you mean, thanks to me?'

Bessie linked arms with Margot, and started leading her away from the gravestones. 'Let's get back home. You's can be making us that coffee … I's can taste it already.'

Margot opened the front door and stopped. She could feel her heart racing, and felt sick. 'I don't know if I can go in, Bessie. Not now. Now Miles is no longer here.'

I'd even be content if he came in the night as a ghost again. Any way is better than not at all.

She swallowed hard and took some deep breaths. It didn't occur to Margot she had nowhere else to go. Not that it mattered one way or another, because Bessie had other ideas. She pushed past and grabbed Margot's hand.

'You's not getting outta making me that coffee, young lady. Come on, I's thinking it will do you's some good, too.' She literally dragged Margot inside.

The strength in Bessie's arms always surprised the younger woman. She couldn't pull away, so she didn't bother trying.

Once over the threshold, Margot stared, wide-eyed at the hall she'd left at least a month ago. Everything was still the way she'd left it. That in itself wasn't a surprise. It was the vase of flowers. They looked as fresh as the day she'd picked them. It was as if she hadn't been away at all.

Bessie watched Margot's face and smiled. 'I's thinking you's mind is a bit boggled. What was you's expecting?'

'I honestly don't know. But one thing stands out that I wasn't expecting, and that's the fresh flowers. I put them there the day before I left. How is that even possible?'

'You's come back at the same time you's left.'

'What? But that's crazy.'

'No, not really. I's thinking everything's as it should be. Come, let's get that coffee.'

Bessie dropped Margot's hand and marched off to the kitchen.

Within a few minutes, they were sitting at the table with a steaming mug of coffee in their hands.

Margot stared at Bessie over the brim of her mug. 'So, are you going to tell me how it was thanks to me Meg fell pregnant? It sounds a bit far-fetched to me,'

Bessie took another sip of her coffee, and sighed. 'I's thinking how much I's missed this.' She gave another sigh and took a long, satisfying sniff at the liquid.

'Bessie. Stop messing about and tell me.'

'Patience is a virtue you's not possessing.' Bessie's lips twitched, then she gave in. 'You's no fun. Okay.' She took one more sip of her coffee, her face an expression of pure bliss, then put the mug down.

Margot put her elbows on the table, rested her chin in her hands, and waited.

Bessie rolled her eyes. 'What was it you's wanted

to know? Oh, yes.' She laughed at Margot's pained expression. 'Miles and Meg's baby. I's thinking it were you's taking over Meg's body that helped stir up her's baby-making bits. She'd been living on her's nerves after her father died. No longer part of society, she thought no one liked her anymore. It messed up her body clock. Learning the truth, it were like she'd been released from some dark place. She got her life back again. Once that happened, she got her's self pregnant straight away. Ladies in thems days thought it were wrong to like it. Meg changed, thanks to you.' Bessie gave another little chuckle. 'I's thinking she were rather surprised how much she's liking it after you's leaving her.'

Margot blushed and turned away to the sound of Bessie's chuckle. 'Well, I'm really pleased for Meg, and I *am* happy they had the long, blissful marriage they deserved.'

But what about my happiness?

'What about Miles' parents, and Gwendolyn and Jenkins? And what about the solicitor, Mr Crankston-Smythe? Did any of them get punished?'

'When Meg went with Miles to confronted them, Jenkins said he would confess to the murders if Gwendolyn was left out of it. Gwendolyn refused to allow it, saying it was all down to her. In the end, Meg couldn't have their deaths on her conscience. Hanging were still the punishment for murder and she's knowing what her brother were like. She asked Miles to forget it. There was no proof, unless they dug the bodies up. I's thinking Meg had a good heart. As for our solicitor, Miles accepted he was bullied into doing what he did. But he retired shortly after and became a recluse.'

'Really? In a way I can understand Miles letting him off. Knowing what his father was like, the poor man didn't have much choice. And what about them? Miles' parents?'

'Miles and Meg went to see them. Meg were no longer the timid girl they knew. You's changed her with the memories you's made and left for her. Miles told them Meg knew what they'd done to her father, and how they'd taken everything from her mother. He told them Meg was willing to forgive them both. But just seeing Meg in her mansion, all of the hatred that Miles' mother had harboured over the years, erupted into something I's couldn't possibly describe. Then she really did have a heart-attack. A big one. There were no saving her. She died in front of them. Lord Brandon lived his life a broken man. There were no point punishing him further.'

'Well at least I know what happened to them all. In a strange way they were all punished. Do you want a coffee refill?'

'Seeing's as you's asking,' Bessie replied, holding out her mug.

The Return

It didn't take Margot long to return to her normal, boring routine, but her heart ached for Miles. She hadn't seen anything of Bessie for days, and that hadn't helped. She missed her company.

Every night, whilst lying in bed, Margot tried to stay awake for as long as possible. She lay there, with tears wet on her cheeks, hoping Miles would come to her again just as he had before. But he never did. He had no reason to.

She phoned into work and asked for more time off, offering to take the rest of the holiday she was owed. But they knew Margot wasn't a shirker and told her to take sick leave.

The cold days and colder nights were keeping Margot indoors. She hadn't the energy to go out. She moped around the house or flopped out on the sofa. She knew she was doing herself no favours and really would be ill if she didn't pull herself together.

It was one such day, when she was sitting idly on the sofa, that a determined knock on the front door startled her. Not expecting anyone, she was rather reluctant to find out who was there. But the visitor knocked again. Margot dragged herself off the sofa and walked to the door,

Irritated that someone would intrude on her misery, she jerked the door open ready to give the person a piece of her mind. Instead, she stared, unable to speak, unable to move.

'Hello, I'm looking for Miss Margot Crawford. Would that be you?' He smiled, his eyes twinkling, approving of what he saw, and Margot's heart flipped.

Margot gripped the door tighter, scared she'd fall if she let go. *How is this possible? It must be a dream.*

She coughed, and a splutter of, 'Yes, that's me,' came out. It didn't sound like her voice at all. 'And who are you?' *Who are you? What a stupid question. It's Miles. It's Miles...*

'Oh, I'm sorry. My name is Miles Brandon, I hope you don't mind me calling on you like this, but I have … Are you all right?' The expression on Miles' face changed from undisguised interest to one of concern. 'You look like you—'

'Miles?' Margot knew she was acting like a prize nincompoop, but she couldn't stop herself.

She wanted to grab him, she wanted to laugh, cry, she wanted to take him upstairs, she wanted…

'I's thinking you's better be letting him in.' Bessie had a mile-wide, satisfied smile on her face. 'This is Miles and Meg's great-grandson.'

Knowing that Bessie had suddenly appeared behind her, didn't faze Margot at all. She was used to her popping up without warning.

'I'm so sorry, Lord Brandon. Please forgive my rudeness. Won't you come in?' She opened the door wider and stood back.

Miles looked surprised. 'How did you know I was Lord Brandon? I hardly ever use my title except when I need to go to London.'

Whoops. 'I didn't know, but you have the air of a lord.' *This is getting worse.* 'Please, do come in before we let all my heat out.' This time Margot smiled and waved him through. 'Go and make yourself comfortable, I won't be a moment.'

When he'd passed her, Margot gave Bessie a quizzical look. It was obvious that Miles hadn't seen her.

'I's thinking you's going to be all right now.' She leaned over and gave Margot a kiss on the cheek. 'This might not be the Miles you's left behind, but this one is just as nice as his great-granddaddy. He's going to be loving you, and this time it will be *you* he loves, Margot. There's not a Meg in sight. You's both going to have a long and very happy life, my dear.' She looked past Margot. 'I's thinking he's waiting for you. Off you's go now.'

Margot turned to look. When she turned back, Bessie had gone.

The End

Sandra Stoner-Mitchell

By the same author
<u>Time Travelling Trilogy:</u>

Bk 1: This Time – Next Time
Bk 2: Beyond That Time
Bk 3: This Time it's Personal

~~~

Betrayal.

~~

<u>For the 8-13s</u>
<u>Eric's Time Travelling Series</u>
Bk 1: Eric and the Aliens
Bk 2: Eric and the Indians
Bk 3: Eric and the Mummies
Bk 4: Eric and the Mermen

~~

'The Return' is the first book
In a new series of time-travelling stories.
Watch out for:
<u>This Time it's Different</u>

Sandra Stoner-Mitchell

Dear readers.

Thank you so much for reading my latest novel. I hope you enjoyed meeting time-travelling Bessie. There will be more with her and another time-traveller, Mildred, from the This Time -That Time, trilogy. Together they will go back in time to stop the future from being changed by people from other timelines.

If you would like to email me about any of my books, please do, I'd be more than happy to answer any questions:

sandramaureenmitchell@gmail.com

To sell our books, authors rely heavily on their readers to leave a review on Amazon. It makes a big difference. If you enjoyed my book enough that you could do that for me, I would be so very grateful, and thank you in advance.

The Return

Sandra Stoner-Mitchell

Printed in Great Britain
by Amazon

22617146R00175